Witches'
Treasure

Part two:
A Witches Tale

Payton Morgan

Contents

Chapter 1

1669

The sound of Mrs. Red's chickens filled Eleanor's room. Her room was on the south side of the house, directly beside the chicken coop, and every day she was the first to be awakened by those damn birds. Her parents, Grace and Henry, would be up and about soon after once the shrieking cocks get to a point where the whole village is awake. The loudest of Mrs. Red's chickens was a rooster she had called Bastard because that's what she would call him when he woke everyone up. She had meant to cook Bastard, but roosters were hard to find, so until she could find one that was not as loud as Bastard, she was stuck with him.

It was a cool October day; Eleanor had placed a couple of logs into the main chimney in the living room and lit it. Since she was the first one up, she always had to start right away with her chores. She peered over at the sink and saw several plates that were still dirty. Her brother Peter was supposed to clean them last night. *That boy, I swear,* she thought. Eleanor marched over to the sink and quickly scrubbed the remaining plates and spoons that were sprawled in the sink. By the time she was done, her father was slowly coming to life behind her.

"Morning, love," he muttered as he kissed the right side of her head.

"Morning, Father; you need to speak with Peter about finishing his chores," she demanded. Henry peered over at the now freshly washed plates and silverware that Eleanor had just gotten done with. He gave an annoyed look as he looked back down the hall at Peter's door.

"Next, be sure to mention that next time I see him," he said. The rest of the house slowly came to life. Peter trudged throughout the living room as if he had walked from here to Boston. Their mother was working over a hangover; she smelt of hot sex as she practically crawled around the house. After breakfast, Eleanor quickly got dressed and ready for school. She had to help Peter get dressed because of how sluggish he was moving. When they were both ready, they made their way out of the house.

***

"H've goo ay," their mother uttered. *God, she's out of it today,* Eleanor thought. She knew what she meant to say was 'Have a good day,' but she still couldn't help but feel sad for her mother. Grace Shrowl was the town whore. If Eleanor had to guess, she had probably slept with almost every man in the village at least once. Another thing that she guessed as well is that Peter is her half-brother. Grace claims by God that he is Henry's child, but he looks more like Paster Drumhold. He had balding brown hair and a mole that took up five percent of his face on the right-hand side. Peter had brown hair, whereas Eleanor was blonde. The village of Florence, Massachusetts, was small but very active. In the town center was the church; surrounding the church were the stables, carpenters, and blacksmiths. Outside of those small establishments were the bakeries and markets that traded resources with the farmers in the area. The rest of the town consisted of over twenty-five homes. Eleanor's was one of the few homes that were farthest from the school. The schoolhouse was located just up the street from the church. Most times, they would learn about the gospels along with their studies. Paster Drumhold had even stopped by a couple of times to preach to us himself. Eleanor didn't much care for school. She always thought that she could learn more by herself than in a classroom. Eleanor loved to read most of all; she enjoyed poetry, and she had read Macbeth four times. She began reading when she was eight, and from then, she could not put a book down since. She had asked her father to get her some paper and quills so that she might write her own stories just like Shakespeare.

The wind was brisk, and she and Peter were now speed-walking to the schoolhouse. They stopped when Peter saw Mr. Harrow, the blacksmith making axes. The smell of smoldering metal and coal filled both her nose as well as Peter's. It was an unpleasant smell, but it was better than the smell of horse shit which she always smelt walking to school. William Farsh, the local pig farmer, always bid them both good morning when he and his son would shovel the shit off the main roads for carriages to get through. She remembered just a week ago, his son Edward had asked to take her out to a picnic he would prepare. Under any circumstances, she would have gone with him, but one thing that boy could never get rid of was the smell of horse and pig shit. You can't be within two feet of either of them without gagging. She and Peter would often hold their breaths every time they walked past them when going to school. They had finally reached the schoolhouse. It was slightly warmer than it was inside due to how many kids were crammed in. The schoolhouse had only three rooms too, a larger room for the older students and a smaller one for the younger ones. The gap in these rooms was nobody under the age of twelve could be with the older students. Everyone else had to go into the smaller room. The last room in the building was an office for the head teacher Mrs. Inkly. She was in charge of disciplining students when they misbehaved. Eleanor had never been to Mrs. Inkly's office before but could only imagine what she would do to other students.

When Eleanor and Peter got inside, they gave a goodbye hug and proceeded to their assigned rooms. In Eleanor's room, there were around ten to fifteen other kids in there all of them ranging in age. Most of the students in this classroom did not care for it. The only one she did like was a fourteen-year-old girl named Greta Toddle. She, unlike the others, was not a nuisance to the class or her. Greta shared Eleanor's love for poetry and her hatred for Eliza Please, who was now officially the oldest student in the school.

"Here comes the harlot's bastard!" Eliza obnoxiously shouted across the room. She and her friends giggled into their hands as Eleanor took her seat in the third row.

"Mind your tongue, Eliza, unless you want to keep it!" Greta snapped sharply. Eliza's grin slowly faded into a scowl. Greta moved from her original spot to the empty seat next to Eleanor's and gently began to comfort her. "Are you okay?" She asked. Eleanor nodded, but in truth, she was not okay. Every time Eliza spoke, it felt like a dagger quickly jabbing at her flesh. Her harsh words would always find a way to creep along with Eleanor as the day progressed. At one point, she had been sent home crying after Eliza and her church friends had called her a "whore in progress." It didn't make that day any better when she saw that her mother had come home with another man while her father was out hunting. That memory, along with the harsh words, still resides and continues to jab at her heart and her soul today.

Sister Ingrid had finally entered the room and ordered the class to settle down and break out their Bibles. Eleanor quickly broke it out and flipped to Corinthians.

"Do not be deceived: 'Bad company corrupts good morals.' 15:33. Could anyone tell me what that means for the class?" Several people raised their hands, and out of all of the people who wanted to answer, Sister Ingrid chose Eleanor to answer. "Ellie? What do you think "Bad company corrupts good morals' mean?" Eleanor did not fully grasp some of the scripture. For her, the Bible was a book full of riddles and hidden meanings that often get misinterpreted by those who read it. Then she looked at Greta, who was smiling and encouraging her. Eleanor had something in mind, but before she could get it out, Eliza stood up and answered for her.

"It means that bad people should be sent away for us to live gracefully in the eyes of the lord. Like Ellie and her heathen family." She blurted. Eleanor's eyes and face began to feel hot, hot with rage. She jerked up and wanted to pounce on Eliza, but before she could, Sister Ingrid beat her to Eliza's seat.

"You watch your tone, Miss Flease, or I will send you home with a red bottom. I do not care if your father is the pastor; I will not tolerate disobedience. Do I make myself clear!" She fumed. Eliza nodded from the side of her face. "DO I MAKE MYSELF CLEAR!!!"

"YES!!!" She replied.

"Good, now apologize to Eleanor."

"m' sry," she murmured.

"Come again; I couldn't hear you?" Sister Ingrid said obnoxiously.

"I'm sorry, Eleanor...." She said with fury in her voice. Eleanor felt as though she was looking straight through her. It was like her eyes were beams of hot light that struck at her soul. Eliza sat back down angrily and continued to stare down Eleanor with that same hot fury. Sister Ingrid got back to Eleanor's desk and asked again.

"What do you think that means, Eleanor?" She had to think about what she was about to say again; her thoughts had been replaced by blind rage. When she finally regathered her thoughts, she answered.

"It means that one must surround oneself with those who lift you up and do away with others who do not; it also means that those that do mean us harm are to be forgotten so that our spiritual morals are kept intact." She said proudly. Sister Ingrid smiled graciously. Behind her, she could hear Eliza scoffing in her corner. Eleanor could still feel her staring at her from the back of her head. That same feeling continued throughout the class.

***

The rest of the class continued like normal; first, they went through the inner workings of several verses about forgiveness and peace. Eleanor believed that Sister Ingrid chose those verses to die down the tension that she and Eliza created. After that, they did some writing; they tried to perfect their cursive writing. While Eleanor did not have a problem writing in cursive, Greta did. Her letters would always find a way to look blocky. It also didn't help that when Greta wrote her hands get according to her "finicky" When Eleanor was done with her exercises, she went over to Greta's desk and helped her guide the quill across the page fluently. Her hand was shaking rapidly in her Eleanor's hand as she wrote. She did her best to try and calm her down by telling her to breathe and to take her time. She even went so far as to breathe along with her just so that she could ease herself at a comfortable pace. Once she did, her handwriting improved. Eleanor felts an immense amount of pride when she saw Greta's face light up at how she was writing. She had finished their exercises much quicker than she normally would.

After everyone was finished, they all turned in their sheets, and that was the end of the school day. School normally lasted about a couple hours for Eleanor, three at the most. When she had gotten outside, she reunited with Peter, and they both, along with Greta, began to walk back home.

The town was now more alive than it was when they walked to the schoolhouse. There were more people out and about going on with their business as they would any other day. The weather had warmed up quite a bit since this morning, so much so that Eleanor did not need to wear her coat. The three of them had passed across the bakery the smell of rolls and buns filled the air. It masked the smell of horse shit elegantly. Which Eleanor greatly appreciated.

They had passed several buildings and were stopped by Jacob Farrow. Unlike Edward Farsh, Jacob was much stockier than he was. He had black smudges on his arms. He had peach fuss surrounding his mouth and cheeks with little bits of black hair poking through. His short black hair looked as though he had not bathed in days. However, it might just be from the black ashy dust that came from forging rifles and axes. Eleanor could feel the raw flaming heat that he had been standing in front of all day just from how close he was to her. She felt a heat rising from her chest from how he approached her as if there was a furnace inside her heart.

"Hi, Ellie!" He said.

"Hi Jacob!" said Peter in response. "What did you make today?"

"Well, my father and I just finished making rounds for the rifles."

"For Mr. Garrett, I assume, right?" Eleanor asked. Jacob nodded; his face quickly popped to life with excitement.

"Oh, I just remembered something! Come see what my father made this morning!" He said excitedly. Eleanor and Greta smiled and gushed at how Jacob was acting. It reminded Eleanor of Peter on his birthday when he was expecting presents. They went into Mr. Farrow's blacksmith's shop, trying to keep up with Jacob. The inside of the shop smelt rustic, and she felt a rising heat around her. Mr. Farrow loved making guns and weapons his personal collection he kept hanging on the walls of his shop. One of his most prized possessions was a golden pistol. Underneath the gun was a label that read 'GODSPEED.' There were many different weapons ranging from small pistols to large rifles. Jacob had everyone go to the back of the shop where his father was out, making yet another round for the long rifles.

"Hi, Mr. Farrow!" Eleanor exclaimed. He looked up quickly and smiled graciously. Mr. Farrow was a heavily built man with a beard that stretched down to his stomach. His arms looked as though they could crush somebody's head with them. His face, while it was covered in black ash, was very friendly and welcoming.

"Miss and Mr. Shrowl, how are you!" He gushed. He looked over at Greta and asked. "And who is this fine young lady?"

"Greta sir, Greta Young," She replied.

"Well, Greta, welcome to my workshop! have you two been back here before?" He asked Eleanor and Peter. They both shook their heads no. Eleanor looked around the workshop to see many anvils and fire pits as well as a large workbench with many different tools. In the middle of the bench was an object wrapped in red velvet. "Well, feel free to watch me make some-"

"Father, if you don't mind, I was hoping you could show them the thing you made for Pastor Please," Jacob asked. Mr. Farrow's face lit up with excitement just as his sons did.

"Ah, yes, of course! You, kids, will love it!" He reached to his workbench and presented the velvet-cloaked object.

Mr. Farrow carefully undid the bindings on it and pulled out a broad silver sword. Eleanor, Greta, and Peter were entranced by the shimmer the blade had. The fire that Eleanor stood next to gazed upon them from the reflection of the blade. It was almost blinding; Mr. Farrow quickly wrapped it back in its velvet cloth and gently put it back on the workbench. "Not bad for me, first sword, heh?" He asked.

"That was your first sword!" Peter exclaimed.

"Yes, lad, and it will probably be the last I only make firearms." Mr. Farrow responded.

"Why? that is a beautiful sword," Eleanor questioned. Before he could answer her question, Paster Flease and Eliza walked into the workshop. Eliza held a handkerchief over her mouth and nose to cover the stench. The pastor was a sickly-looking man who looked as though his skin was made of parchment. He was much taller than Mr. Farrow, but he was half his weight. The pastor presented himself as if he were royalty as he entered the workshop.

"Ah, Pastor, how are you?" Mr. Farrow asked politely.

"My sword Walter is it ready?" His voice sounded as though he had smoked half his life. This sent a chill right down Eleanor's spine. Mr. Farrow looked somewhat frightened by the pastor as he spoke. He quickly presented the sword to him, and the pastor practically swiped it out of his hand. He wrapped the sword and examined it. Checking all the angles and the sharpness of the blade itself. "Yes... this will do just nicely," He hissed. The Pastor peered over at Eleanor and the others. "What are they doing in here?"

"They came in to see the sword, sir," Mr. Farrow answered.

"Did those two touch it?" He seethed, pointing at both Eleanor and Peter. Mr. Farrow growing angrier, approached the pastor slowly.

"What if they did?" He snapped.

"I do not want unholy hands on my weapon Walter."

"We did not touch it, Pastor," Eleanor blurted. The pastor gazed into Eleanor's eyes. His gaze was far worse than Eliza's. This was a crazed maddening stare of uncut rage. The pastor stood over both her and Peter and smirked.

"Good... then let this be a lesson. Do not touch my holy weapon of faith. Or I will bring down God's wrath on your child."

"That's enough, Pastor; just take the damn sword and go," Mr. Farrow interjected. The pastor leered at Mr. Farrow and gave him the same blank maddening stare he gave Eleanor. "NOW!" he shouted. Both the Pastor and Eliza trudged out of the workshop.

"Are you okay?" Mr. Farrow asked Eleanor and Peter. He nodded, but Eleanor did not.

***

Greta, Peter, and Eleanor slowly exited Mr. Farrow's shop with Jacob accompanying them. All of them remained silent as they walked out. Peter looked as though he was about to cry; Eleanor held him tightly so that he wouldn't. Greta was fuming. She had wanted to say something, but fear had gripped her vocal cords when the pastor was present. Eleanor tried her best to keep her composure and remain calm. Right now, all she wanted to do was go home and cry. Before they could head off, Jacob stopped them.

"Sorry about that. I should have to guess the Pastor would have come for his sword."

"It's okay," Eleanor lied.

"It's not okay! How dare he say those things! The bastard!" Greta shouted. Eleanor slowly calmed her down. "And what does a pastor need with a silver sword?" Both Eleanor and Greta looked at Jacob curiously.

"He likes to go hunting with the other farmers. He likes to feel the animals as they pass on into heaven. He says"

"That is sick!" Eleanor said disgustedly.

"I agree," Jacob concurred. There was an awkward silence between the four of them.

"Well, we better get going; father would be expecting us by now," Eleanor said. Peter nodded; it seemed as though all his happiness was stripped away by the Pastor's menacing presence.

"I should get home as well; you sure all is well?" Greta asked again. Eleanor nodded. "Well, if you need anything, you know where to find me," she said as she strolled back to her house. Before Eleanor could begin her walk back home, Jacob grabbed her arm gently.

"Ellie, I'm sorry; let me make this right."

"It's alright, Jacob, I promise."

"Come to the river behind Johnson's farm at twilight tonight," He asked.

"What, why?"

"Just come, please," He begged. Everything in her was telling her not to indulge him, but then she saw how sincere he was, and her heart melted all over again.

"Fine," She said, smiling."

"See you then" Both Peter and Eleanor made their way back home.

Chapter 2

The Salt-Watered Pond

Eleanor had waited until it was twilight outside before leaving the house. She crept throughout the house, making sure the wood floors would not creak at her footsteps. She was nearly caught by her mother, who was half-conscious in the rocking chair next to the nearly dead fireplace. Eleanor gently grabbed a blanket her grandmother had woven and placed it over her. She nearly gagged at the smell of her drunken mother. It was overpowering her desire to kiss her forehead goodnight.

When Eleanor successfully covered her mother, she walked carefully out of the house and to Johnson's farm. She made sure when she left the house that she layered up. She had on three jackets along with long pairs of pants and socks. Even with the extra layers, the wind was brutal. It cut through her clothing and sent her into a shivering fit. She quickly made her way over to Johnson's farm. Their lanterns were still lit. Eleanor waited for a couple of minutes until the lanterns went dim, and Farmer Johnson went to bed. She crept alongside the left-hand side of the farm carefully. The full moon had lit up the night sky; she felt as though she did not need her lantern. The only thing that she could hear in the dead of night was the sound of crickets. As she moved closer into the woods where the riverbank was, she could hear something else. It sounded like there were people out here. Multiple people. *Did he invite more people?* While she was a little disappointed that it was not going to be just them out here, she did feel some comfort that there were others in case she got lost. She grew closer to the woods, trying her best not to trip over rocks or tree roots. There was a slight hint of fog in the woods; the trees looked as though they were planted in straight rows and columns; however, the foliage made it difficult to navigate through it.

She heard the people talking and laughing more now, along with the sound of her feet crushing the leaves beneath her. When she finally made it to the river, she saw a roaring fire and about twenty other kids her age there. Some of them were dancing around the fire; others were talking amongst themselves. She spotted Jacob out of the group of guys and girls dancing around the fire. His face lit up when he saw her, and Eleanor's face felt warm when they locked eyes. He ran to her and hugged her tightly; a warm feeling traveled throughout her chest and stomach.

"So glad you could come, Ellie!" He said.

"Jacob, what is this?" She asked. Jacob wrapped his arm around her shoulder and presented the festivities as if they were some presentation.

"This is my birthday party" Eleanor's eyes bulged, and a slight sense of guilt overcame her.

"Oh my goodness, I had no idea! I should have brought you something!" She said excitedly.

"You coming here is a good enough gift!" Eleanor blushed harder than she had ever blushed before.

Eleanor spent hours dancing and drinking rum with Jacob and several other boys from neighboring towns. She had not had this much fun in a long time. The last thing that she could recall this much fun was when her father took them to a nearby lake during the summer several years ago. She remembered splashing in the water without caring about anything. Eleanor remembered how happy Peter was as well. He, too, could not hold his excitement then again; he was at the ripe age of four, so his excitement was tripled during that little trip. Eleanor felt that same level of excitement as she drank more and more. *I see why mother likes this now;* she thought as she finished off a bottle. She could see a couple of kids kissing each other vigorously. She saw others remove their clothing. She had not seen another girl with her top off before, and she quickly regretted it when she realized it was Eliza. Eleanor felt sick just by that glance at her washboard of a chest. One could easily mistake her for a boy just by looking at her chest. *I'd hate to be her husband.* Eleanor looked down at her chest and smiled at how much larger her breast was than Eliza's. *No wonder she's such a bitch. She's flatter than a goddamn washboard!*

She giggled and hiccupped violently. She hiccupped again. This time she could feel something inside her stomach start to rise like a geyser. Eleanor quickly ran away from the fire and away from everyone else. She vomited on a pine tree she rested on. Her throat felt hot and acidic, and that feeling tripled with each heave. She could feel the vomit dripping off her lips as they fell onto the damp leaves on the ground. Tears began to grace her face as she vomited more.

After what felt like an hour of vomiting, she finally felt somewhat decent. She looked around and saw there was a large log that was sitting on its side. Eleanor looked graciously at the sky. The stars sparkled and shined as if they were angels lighting up the atmosphere. That's what her father would say that the stars were beautiful angels, singing endlessly throughout the night. She remembered how he would cup his ear and say, 'Listen to them sing' All she heard was the crickets chirping. But for a four-year-old girl, that sounded like angels harmonizing. The crickets were chirping once again. It filled her ears and warmed her heart a little. However, that might just be the rum.

"Are you okay, Ellie?" a familiar voice asked. Eleanor looked back and saw that it was Jacob. She smiled and nodded. Jacob saw the fresh vomit next to the tree and sat next to Eleanor. "You got something on your face, Ellie," he said just before he pulled out a handkerchief. He wiped off the left side of her mouth gently.

"Thank you," she said. They both shared a nice silence as they both looked at the stars together. "They're beautiful, aren't they?"

"Indeed they are," he said tenderly. Eleanor could feel as though he was looking at her when he said that. Her skin felt itchy and cold; she shivered slightly. Jacob, without question, gave Eleanor his jacket. She nodded to him, silently thanking him.

"How old are you now, Mr. Farrow?" She asked sarcastically. Jacob chuckled, and so did Eleanor.

"Eighteen"

"Very nice, you're all grown up."

"Yeah... all grown up..." He mumbled. Eleanor could see on his face that he was not fully excited for his turn to adulthood.

"What troubles you, Jacob?" She asked.

"I am to be wed this week; father says that it is time for me to start my own family...." Eleanor felt her heart sink to her stomach as he spoke. She felt itchy again, though not of Jacob but of the shock of this news.

"What? To whom?" Jacob looked back at the fire, and so did Eleanor. In plain view, they both saw Eliza still dancing around the fire topless. Eleanor's sadness quickly changed to rage. The same rage she felt earlier from both schools and when she ran into the pastor. "You cannot be serious?"

"It's true... the pastor and my father had agreed last week."

"She's more of a harlot than my mother; you cannot marry her!" She demanded.

"There's nothing I can do,"

"There is always something you can do. You are grown, and you do not have to abide by what your father or that bastard of a pastor has to say." There was a quick silence again. "There is always another choice, and if you do not want to marry that," she said, pointing at Eliza disgustedly. "Then you do not have to" Silence rang again between them; the only other sound that was present was the sound of the crickets. He nodded and smiled at Eleanor.

"Thank you"

"Of course" They both looked up at the stars again. Then back at each other, Eleanor felt her heart pounding as she looked into his hazel eyes. "Can I ask you something?"

"Anything"

"Why did you invite me here?" He hesitated when answering. Jacob looked a little choked up to answer her question.

"Well, I thought you might need this to try and take your mind off of what happened earlier and as an apology for that as well."

"I appreciate it, Jacob; thank you, this is splendid."

"That and I enjoy your company," He blurted. Eleanor blushed; she felt her heart skip a beat when he spoke. She smiled back at him.

"As do I," she said tenderly. Jacob put his hand on Eleanor's. He had rough skin, and his hands were cold, but they slowly warmed as they embraced each other. Eleanor looked deeply into Jacob's eyes once again; she couldn't help but smile at how his perfect cheekbones and smile made her feel lighter than air. That feeling was killed by the sound of one of Jacob's male friends shouting.

"JACOB, COME JOIN US, MY FRIEND!!!" He shouted. Jacob chuckled again and gave Eleanor a loving gaze.

"You are sure you're alright?" He asked.

"I'll be fine, Jacob; go enjoy yourself" He smiled and rushed back to the bonfire. Eleanor still had his jacket wrapped around her. She could still smell his musk of ash on the jacket. Eleanor looked back at the sky and said.

"Thank you, God, thank you."

"God won't save you now, you dirty whore!" Eliza said as she pressed a knife behind her back.

***

Eliza walked Eleanor further into the hooded darkness of the woods, away from the bonfire. The small dagger that she pressed against Eleanor jabbed her slightly. She could feel as though it had pierced her skin. A small trickle went down her spine down to her waist. It, along with the unforgiving wind, made her colder than she was before. Eliza had taken Jacob's jacket and wrapped it around herself. She was now wearing only that, as well as a small skirt. Eleanor's heart was pounding like crazy; she felt as though it was going to burst out of her chest. *She's going to kill me...* she thought. Eleanor's mind was scattered with different escape routes. However Eliza was much taller than she was, and she was faster as well. The thought of her flipping the dagger back on her came as well. But Eliza could overpower her; while she was fast, she was not as strong as Eleanor.

They both walked for about five minutes until Eliza was sure nobody could hear them. She had the blade pressing against her back while her other hand was on Eleanor's shoulder. Eliza's hands were like ice which suited her due to how coldblooded she and her family were. They both stopped walking as they made their way to a small pond. The pond itself reflected the starry night above. *Oh god, she's going to kill me and then put my body in the water!!!* She began to breathe heavily again at this realization. Her heart was beating a million miles an hour. She didn't know what to do. Eliza then kicked the back of her knees, and Eleanor dropped down with all her weight. She was now on the bank of the pond. Eliza then grabbed a handful of Eleanor's hair and gently graced the blade across her cheek.

"It's not wise to fuck with me whore" Eliza spoke. Eleanor couldn't breathe because of how close Eliza's face was to hers. "Jacob is mine, you filthy little bitch, and if you ever come near him again, I will slaughter you like the pig you are!" She hissed.

"Eliza, please, I promise I won't," Eleanor cried. Eliza let out a slight smile and laughed. It was high-pitched, and she snorted several times during this fit of laughter. Then her face slowly grimaced again; she smiled menacingly.

"I know you won't," She whispered. Eleanor felt a large jab to her stomach; she let out an agonizing scream which was then muffled by Eliza's hand covering it. "Because you will already be dead" Eliza twisted the dagger into Eleanor's stomach. Eleanor coughed up blood as Eliza pulled it out of her. Eliza then pushed Eleanor into the pond; the water was colder than the wind. Eleanor could not see too well in this light. She felt the blood pooling out of her stomach. She had tried to regain herself with just one hand, and the other was clutching her stomach.

"He-help! Help me, please, God help me! "She cried out as loud as she could. The only one who did hear her was Eliza, who was now washing off the blood on her hands and the dagger. Eleanor tried to kick the water beneath her to try and make her way to the shore, but she had lost too much blood. She began to feel dizzy and disoriented. Every part of her body was now shivering profusely. She tried her best to fight through the dizziness, but it was too late. She had lost too much blood, and she slowly descended into the watery depths below.

***

Water pooled into Eleanor's lungs as she tried, again and again, to get above the water, but the work had been done. Eleanor was going to die, and there was nothing she could do about it. Her mind quickly changed from possible escape plans to acceptance of her circumstances. She thought back about how Peter and her parents would think when they found out. That is if they found out. The lake was in the middle of nowhere; they would not find her body. Eleanor opened her eyes beneath the water she saw how her blood mixed with the water around her. Like ink in a bottle, it spread across the entire pond. Eleanor felt her death was nigh, and with that in mind, she released the last bit of air she held onto. Her body convulsed violently; she felt as though her head was about to explode her arms and legs had gone completely numb. Eleanor's convulsions died down slowly as she descended upwards from the lake. Eleanor Shrowl was dead.

***

Eleanor expected that she was going to be greeted at God's pearly white gates; instead, she was transported to the town square. She could see the town's people gathering in the church. Within the crowd of people, she spotted Jacob and his father. Both of them had their best clothes on. They both walked grimly to the church where the rest of the people were walking. Eleanor rushed in front of them to try and speak with them.

"Jacob, what's going on?" She asked. He did not respond. He had not noticed her at all. It was as if he did not know she was there. Eleanor waved her hand over his face a couple of times. She then snapped her fingers right at his face. No response. *Oh God am I a specter?* she thought. Then she looked back at the events that had just unfolded she could be. But that did not answer the question of why she was here. She walked alongside both Jacob and his father to the church. They both weaved through the crowd and took their seats on the second row to the right of the church. At the altar was Pastor Flease, and behind him were several choir girls, one of whom was Eliza. Eleanor went up to where she stood; she was looking for her killer dead between the eyes. Fury raged through her blood and her bones. She spat on Eliza's face, but she didn't notice, just like the rest of the people who trolled into the church.

"Today marks a tragic day, for one of our own has passed." He spoke, seeming to care slightly. Eleanor looked back, and in front of the Pastor was an open coffin. Eleanor looked at both the Pastor and the coffin, confused. From this angle, Eleanor was unable to see who was in the coffin. But she had an idea who it was. *This is my funeral, isn't it?* She looked out into the crowd and saw in the front row Peter who was crying. She saw Jacob, who was sitting behind him, grab his shoulder gently as he, too, was in tears. Eleanor did not see her mother or her father in the crowd. She did see Greta sitting next to Peter, who was also sharing the sadness. Eleanor slowly walked around to get a better look at who was in the coffin. Her heart was pounding like crazy with each step she took. When she reached a point where she could see who was in the coffin, she closed her eyes and took a deep breath. Eleanor opened her eyes, and her rapidly beating heart practically fell to her stomach at what she saw. Eleanor looked upon her cold, lifeless body and began to form tears. She looked back at the crowd and saw that her mother was now sitting next to Peter, crying along with him.

"How can this be? I'm dead."

"Not yet, you're not," a voice said overhead. Eleanor thought it to be God; however, this was of a woman. She never thought that God could be a woman a little part of her was questioning if it was God at all. Eleanor felt a warmness start to rise from her stomach. It was a familiar warmness, the kind she felt when she was throwing up rum. It rose rapidly until it exploded out from her mouth and onto the floor. The contents of what she threw up looked to be just water. She let in a deep breath and vomited again.

***

More water came from her mouth, only this time Eleanor was now on her side when she vomited. Her eyes were watering, and her mouth was dripping with saliva. She was cold and wet, and she was no longer at her mother's funeral. Instead, she was on the bank of the pond. It was now daytime; it was slightly warmer than yesterday, but she was still shivering by how wet she was. She stood up very carefully. She felt lightheaded, and she fumbled a few times, trying to steady herself. When she finally managed to stand up, she looked at herself in the reflection the pond gave off in the sunlight. Eleanor looked pale compared to her naturally tanned skin, she saw that her lips were slightly blue, and her eyes looked as though they receded into her skull. She crouched down over the water and cupped her hands to try and get a drink. When she pours the water down into her mouth, she immediately spits it back up. The water tasted acidic and bitter. She licked the sides of her mouth and tasted something distinct. *This is salt water,* she thought. She looked down and saw that her clothes were free of blood stains. She pulled up her shirt to see how bad the stab wound was, but there was none to be seen. Her skin was smooth, and there seemed to be no trace of any wound to be seen. *Maybe I had too much to drink? No, I felt Eliza's dagger pierce my belly, but how could there be no wound, and how am I still alive?* She pondered, stood back up again, and began to walk away from the pond and to the woods where she came from. Just twenty paces away from the pond was a book that lay on the ground. This book was much larger than any of the books that Eleanor had seen; not only that, but it was heavier than the other books as well. The book looked to be bound in some sort of brown leather; it had stitches across several of its corners. She looked inside, and the lake began to shimmer slightly when she did so. The lake gave off a blueish hue that Eleanor had never seen before. She closed the book, and the hue from the pond had vanished. She opened it again, and so did the blueish hue. Her jaw dropped at this discovery. She had wanted to experiment more, but the wind had picked up once again. She was shivering up a storm with that she took the book and began her journey home.

Chapter 3

Dreaded Discovery

The book that she held felt as though it was moving in her hands. Not so much to be sliding out of her grasp but just enough to where she would notice. It felt as though it was a cat purring, only this was far from a cat. Eleanor looked at this book, both confused and slightly scared of what kind of power this thing had. What she was even more curious about was the fact that her stab wound from Eliza was completely healed. She remembered just how much pain she felt when Eliza jabbed her in the stomach. That is a sensation she will never forget. She looked back at where it was and could not see any sort of wound, not even a scratch. One thing that she did see was a small white flake. She dabbed it with her finger and put it in her mouth. *Salt, just like the lake. How can that be? I know for a fact that the lake did not have salt in it when Eliza shoved me in there. Or was it there before, and I didn't notice?* Eleanor had walked almost half a mile. She did not know exactly where she was; what she did know was that Florence is east, and she learned in school that the sun rises in the east and sets in the west. It had to be around ten or eleven by now, so she decided to follow where the sun looked to be. She had been walking for a solid twenty minutes, shivering as she walked closer and closer to know; she prayed.

Eleanor had tried recalling last night's events so that she could fully understand what had happened to her. She remembered her throwing up from the rum, then Eliza marching her to the lake and stabbing her. She knew for a fact that she was not able to swim to the bank. *But how did I get there?* Then there was the dream of her funeral and the voice she heard in the dream. At first, she thought it was God speaking to her; she remembered how Eliza and her friends kept saying in class that God had to be a woman because a man could not have built such a beautiful world for us to live in. While much truth was in that statement, there was one thing she did not think of. God has a name, Jehovah, which, last time Eleanor checked, was a man's name. She always had to be the one to state that fact in class, which many people agreed with, except for Eliza.

"That evil little—" Eleanor blurted before calming herself. "In time, in time, that little bitch will get what's coming to her." Eleanor thought back again; *after the dream, I woke up on the bank where this was,* she thought, looking down at the book which still purred in her hands. Eleanor opened it again; it did not glow just like it did at the lake she flipped through some of the pages. It looked as though the ink was somewhat fresh. There were several pictures inside this book. Some of which were goats and people and otherworldly creatures she had never seen before. There was some strange writing around some of these pictures, along with regular English writing on other pages. Eleanor looked at the page just behind the cover and saw a passage in the middle of the page.

This book is the property of Morganna Starr.

Morganna Starr? Who the hell is—she heard a rustling of leaves. Someone was close. She found a tree and ducked behind it. The rustling began to be louder and louder until, finally, they stopped cold. Eleanor was still shivering from the cold. She tried to will her body to stop so that whoever it did not hear her. She even covered her mouth to silence her breaths. The silence was deafening; all that was there were the sounds of the wind brushing the leaves. She stood there pondering who or what it could be. *It sounded like a person; there was no gallop in their step or multiple feet sounds. It has to be a person. Maybe it's Eliza checking to see if the job was done. The next time I see that little bitch I'm going to tear her limb from limb.* Eleanor peaked around the tree and spotted a woman. She seemed much older than her, mid-thirties at best. She had long black hair with peaks of grey poking through. She wore a black dress that was very loosely woven; Eleanor was able to see her legs through the skirt of the dress. The dress itself had odd patterns on it, sparkly patterns that she had never seen on a dress before. They were very intricate and detailed. Some looked like stars; others looked like crescent moons. The woman also had a large brown jacket wrapped around her that looked to be fine leather.

SNAP!!

Eleanor quickly looked down and saw that she had accidentally stepped on a branch. She then continued to hide behind the tree. She heard the crunching leaves move closer and closer to her. Her heart began to pound nonstop; she covered her mouth again so she wouldn't make any noise. Eleanor quickly hid the book in her blouse and stood there waiting for whoever this woman was to eventually find her.

***

"Excuse me, madam?" the woman asked. Eleanor let out a scream and fell to the ground, surprised and terrified. She didn't know why she was so terrified of this woman, but something inside told her she should be. I mean, what kind of woman would be out in the middle of the woods at ten in the morning? "Oh my heavens, forgive me, I did not mean to startle yo—" she cut herself off when she got a better look at Eleanor's condition. "My god, you're sopping wet; you must be freezing" The woman quickly took off her jacket and handed it to Eleanor, who was hesitant to take it. "I'm not gonna bite cha, love," she said in a soothing voice. Against her better judgment, Eleanor took the jacket and wrapped it around herself. The inside of the jacket was fleece which felt extremely warm against her skin. "What's your name, love?" the woman asked.

"Eleanor, but most people call me Ellie," she responded through the shivers.

"Nice to meet you, Ellie; I'm Delilah Sharp," she said while reaching out for a handshake. Eleanor took her hand, which was just as warm and comforting as the jacket. "Let's get you somewhere where it's warm. Would you like that, Ellie?"

"Yes, please," she responded. Delilah then stood up and began to walk north of the woods with Eleanor by her side.

***

The walk to her cabin was not long. It had to be about twenty minutes. It was silent; while Eleanor did not quite exactly enjoy the silence, something about it was a little comforting. She did not fully encapsulate the beauty that surrounded her, how the leaves had changed from their bright green colors to auburn, orange, and red with glimpses of yellow. With the wind crashing against the foliage, the treetops looked like fire, a comforting fire, the kind of fire one could cozy up to after a long day. She remembered the last time she had done such a thing not too long ago. Peter had been playing with his toys, and he fell asleep in front of the fire. Eleanor remembered that she had placed a blanket over him and herself as she cuddled Peter in the heat of the fireplace. One thing that was certain was that Eleanor was ready to go home and see Peter again. Along with her father, her mother would probably not even know she was gone in the first place. When Eleanor gets home, the first thing she does is go to the Pastor's house and kick the ever-living shit out of Eliza for what she did to her. Her morals were shot at this point, all because of a stupid boy!!! *A stupid boy that we can't stop thinking about,* she thought.

"Here we are, Ellie," Delilah said with pride. She had been taken to a small cabin, which looked very old and run down. This cabin had tinted windows as if they were lightly brushed with ink on the inside. Delilah opened the doors of her home to Ellie, and she graciously went inside. The cabin was very warm, just like Eleanor's house. It, too, had a fireplace which she spotted instantly and rushed to it. "Wait here, Ellie. I'll be right back." Eleanor nodded and continued to warm herself up in the fire. The cabin alone was casual. There was a troth filled with water for Delilah to wash her hands. The cabin was very well carpeted; one could hardly see the hardwood floors underneath. There were china plates all along the kitchen walls, some of which had pictures of kittens and sunrises on them. The cabin gave off a comfortable feeling of security. This made Eleanor feel much safer than she did when she was walking back from the pond. Eleanor felt the book vibrate slightly in her blouse. She took it out and looked upon it again. It was beginning to glow that same bluish glow that came from the pond. The book felt warm in her hands as she held it. Eleanor heard the creaking of the wood floors in the other room and quickly put the book back into her blouse. Delilah came in with a fresh set of clothes.

"Here we are. I hope they fit all right; they were mine whenever I was your age. You can change into my room if you want."

"Thank you, Delilah," Eleanor spoke softly as she grabbed the clothes and proceeded to the other room. Delilah's room was blander than the front room; there was a small closet and a twin bed there was a large full-body mirror that stood in the corner of her room. Eleanor quickly got undressed and looked fully at her naked body in the mirror; as she checked earlier, there was not a single scratch on her abdomen. She brushed her hands down from her breasts to her hips to see if there was any kind of evidence to suggest otherwise. Nothing. One thing that she did notice was that her skin felt soft, granted it had just been reheated by the fire. But it had never been this soft. Before last night her skin was always dry; she would always have to pour water on her arms in the morning because of how dry they felt. Her body felt rejuvenated, rehydrated, and reborn. She plopped the book onto the bed and put on the clothes that Delilah had given to her. Thankfully they fit barely. The shirt had a large V-neck which, with the size of her breasts, could pop out if she wasn't careful. The skit was a brownish red which she did not mind at all. One thing that she did mind was that Delilah did not have any bra with it. She could tell that Delilah was not wearing any bra when she found her in the woods, so Eleanor assumed that she did not own any. She couldn't blame her; she remembered the days she had when she first had to use one and the rash it caused on her chest. Eleanor was not going to go around with soggy undergarments, so she just decided to do away with them. *I'll get some when I go home,* she thought. She felt something brush against her neck suddenly. She looked behind her at Delilah's closet. There was something different about this closet that she could not place. It had two intertwined wooden doors, both of which looked homemade. *I could have sworn I felt something; she* thought as she reached closer to the closet. She then heard a knocking on the door.

"You okay in there?" Delilah asked.

"Just fine," Eleanor responded. She then grabbed the book, stuck it in her blouse again, and walked out with her soggy clothes. "Where do you—"

"Just set them in that basket next to the door." Eleanor did what she was told. She then went back into the living room and sat down on one of the chairs next to the fire. Delilah came in and gave her a cup of tea; Eleanor nodded as she sat down across from her.

"Thank you again, Delilah."

"Not a problem, deary" Eleanor looked around and admired the cabin once again.

"I assume you and your husband live here?" She asked.

"Oh no, dear, it's just me. I built all of this myself. Men who need em'" She chuckled. Eleanor followed.

"You live here all by yourself?"

"Why yes, just listen with me," she said as she cupped her hand around her left ear.

"I don't hear anything."

"EXACTLY!!!" Delilah laughed again. "All there is here is the sweet sounds of nature, and that, to me, is all I need." Eleanor smiled as she sipped her tea. "Now, you mind telling me why you were out here sopping wet and clearly hiding something in your blouse?" Eleanor was shocked by both her language and her question. "It's alright, you can show me," Delilah said compassionately. Eleanor pulled out the book and showed it to Delilah.

"I found this in the woods. I don't know exactly what it is," Eleanor said as she handed it to Delilah. She examined it closely for a few seconds. Delilah shook her head in defeat.

"I have never seen anything like this before, and who's this, Morganna Starr?"

"No idea"

"I see, but that still doesn't explain why you were out there," Eleanor was hesitant to tell her the details of what happened, mostly because she didn't know exactly how she ended up out of the pond in the first place.

"Well... there was this boy."

"DID HE HURT YA? HE AND I WILL HAVE A GO—" Delilah shouted.

"NO, no, he didn't hurt me, but someone who liked him did; this little bitch in class named Eliza."

"The pastor's daughter?"

"You've heard of her; yeah, from what I see, she's as unholy as that damn pastor" Eleanor nodded in agreement. "So, what exactly happened between you two?" Eleanor explained all that she could remember without disclosing the vision she had about her funeral. She also left out that Eliza stabbed her; she instead told Delilah that Eliza grabbed a large rock, knocked her out, and then tossed her in the pond nearby. Eleanor also told her how the book appeared to her by the pond. She didn't seem to care; she was focused on Eliza. "Why that evil little—"

"I know; I'll get her back, I swear."

"If you won't, I will," Delilah added. "Though nobody would take the word of a lonely old woman in the woods."

"Why not?"

"Just a moment ago, you assumed I was married; what good is one woman's word if the woman in question has no spouse, especially talking about something like this? They would accuse me of what you said before the pastor's daughter." That realization did not fully materialize for Eleanor until just now. Nobody would believe her if she didn't have anyone else to back it up with. *I could tell Jacob or Greta, and they'd believe me.*

"Can you tell me how to get back to town?" Eleanor asked. Delilah simply got up and handed Eleanor a parchment that had a small map of the county they were in.

"If you take the path that we were on and turn left at right at the median, you will find a gravel path; that path will lead you straight to town, though it is a couple of hour walk from here. And it is getting dark out."

"Please, I must get home and see my parents."

"Very well, if you are going out, at least take this as well," Delilah said while handing Eleanor a warm fleece jacket.

"Oh no, I can't," she said kindly.

"Take it. " she said, handing the jacket and the book to her.

"Thank you for everything, Delilah; how can I repay you?"

"Just get home safe for me, okay?"

"I will," Eleanor said just before leaving the cabin and trekking out into the woods again.

***

It was sunset, and the woods began to come alive with crickets and lightning bugs. It looked as though it was going to rain. But that did not matter to Eleanor; what did matter was that she made it back home to her parents. Hopefully, something could be done about her attack last night. *Eliza will pay,* she thought as she made her way through the path to the median. The breeze sent chills down Eleanor's back, which caused her to put Delilah's jacket on and pull the hood over her head. It was a full moon, and the light shined through the trees dimly. It was as though the moon was lighting the path in which Eleanor needed to go. Eleanor was now alone with her thoughts again. Though on the plus side, at least she wasn't soaking wet, nor was she hurt (from what she could gather). The walk to the median took less time than what Delilah said. She had reached the median in what felt like thirty minutes. She turned left, and sure enough, there was a path. Eleanor marched on just as Delilah said. The path she was on now was more lit up than her previous one. It was in the direct direction of the moon, and Eleanor was walking down a lonely road. She looked to her left and right, and all she could see was darkness with just peaks of moonlight.

She pulled out the book and continued walking down this path; she had to hold the book close to her face to make out any sort of writing that was scribbled on it. Eleanor held it out into the moonlight, and the book was almost as clear as one was reading it during the day. There were several pictures of goats and skulls. She flipped through a couple of pages and found one page where a topless woman was burning at the stake; there were some odd symbols and words written around the picture. She flipped through the book more and found a page that had nothing, but those odd words written, listed in alphabetical order. On the right-hand side of these pages were real words.

Gratis lostrus – light

"What could that mean?" Eleanor spoke to herself. She looked around and read from the book "Gratis lostrus" instantly; the pages of the book began to glow that same bluish glow she saw from the lake and when she first held the book. Eleanor dropped the book and yelped. She stared blankly at the book that still was glowing on the ground in front of her. She felt a mixture of both heart and curiosity when gazing at the book. Eleanor had never seen anything like this before, *since when does a book glow? What do I do? Leave it? Pick it up?* She inched closer and closer to the glowing book and carefully picked it back up. She opened it again, and sure enough, she was now able to read from the book with ease. She looked at another word she found on the same page she was on just moments ago. She read aloud again; this time, she closed her eyes as she did so. "Undos," just like the last time she read from the book, the book's glow slowly dimmed, and she was left in the darkness; yet again, her only source of light was the pale moonlight. She looked around again and read the same spell again. "Gratis Lostrus," the book instantly glowed that same extravagant glow it gave off before. Eleanor's eyes bulged widely at this discovery; she could not believe it, but here it was in her hands. A spell book.

***

Eleanor continued her walk into town; she was determined to get back home and show Peter the book. He would eat this up, a magic book that can do whatever one's heart desires. The pages of the book lit up to where Eleanor could read them perfectly without any sort of problems with how dark it was outside. She went down the list and found one she thought looked promising. But before she could read it, she heard the rumble of the clouds and the trickling of rain around her. She looked up at the sky, and sure enough, it started to rain. Eleanor stashed the book back into her blouse and proceeded to walk much faster than she had before. Ten minutes had gone by of her walking, and she was still completely dry. Yet she can hear the rain pounding in the trees. Eleanor stuck her hand out, and she did not feel a single drop of rain fall upon it.

She pulled out the book and read "Gratis Lostrus" again; the book lit up once again and revealed that there was now a circle about two feet in diameter around her. Outside of the circle, the rain kept coming down. She took a step towards the outer rim of the circle, but just as she took that one step, the circle surrounding her moved with her. She looked at the book, then back at the sky. "The book is protecting itself?" she questioned. Eleanor pushed that thought away and continued walking; she still used the book as a source of light. It was at this point now that not even the moon could guide her path home. She had walked for another thirty minutes, and at that point, she saw the large sign that stood out at the very edge of town. She closed the book and undid the light spell she read when she walked through. Finally, after a night of hell and mystery, she was now home in Florence.

***

When walking through the roads of the town, it appeared different from what she had seen just yesterday. It seems as though there were more houses than there were before. Then again, it is almost dinner time now, so it might just be the lack of light. One thing that Eleanor hated about Florence was that there were no street signs; then again, there are only three or four "streets" (if you want to call them that) in Florence. She remembered her street always had a large pine tree at the corner entering the street. She remembered decorating that tree one year for Christmas with Peter.

"Oh my, Peter..." she said to herself as she made her way down the road again. Thankfully the light outside of her house was still on. She knew it was her house by how old it was. Father was not the best craftsman when he built this house just before she and Peter were born. Eleanor smelt a familiar smell of pork which was very uncommon for a father to make. She went up to the porch and knocked, expecting Peter or her father to answer. Instead, it was a small girl and a blonde-haired woman. This somewhat shocked Eleanor when she saw them.

"Can I help you?" the kind woman asked.

"Uh, sorry, I think I got the wrong house," Eleanor responded. "I thought the Shrowl's lived here."

"Shrowl's? Oh, you must mean the family that used to live here" Eleanor's eyes bulged at this news.

"What do you mean used to live here?" Eleanor questioned. "They don't live here anymore?"

"Nope, not since their daughter died last year" Eleanor's heart sank into her stomach when she heard the woman speak.

"L-l-last year?"

"Mmm hmm, darn shame drowned in a lake as far as I know" Eleanor could not believe what she was hearing; it was something out of a nightmare, something so crazy and delusional to even conceive. *No, no, no, there's no way I've been gone for a year!!!* She thought hysterically. Eleanor looked into the woman's eyes; she looked as though she was giving her God's honest truth; Eleanor's heart sank lower and lower into the pits of her soul. *Oh my god.*

"Are you okay, lady?" said the little girl. Eleanor didn't know what else to do, so she marched away from the door without answering her.

***

Her march turned into a run, which then turned into a sprint into one of the only other buildings she knew in the town. Mr. Farrow's blacksmith's shop. The door was locked, and she managed to break the front window and crept inside. The fire was still warm, so she managed to muster whatever warmth that was left in the once-set blaze. She looked around again and lit a lantern that was left on the front counter of the shop. The shop itself looked newer than it did when she last entered here (a year ago).

"This doesn't make any sense; how have I been gone for a year? A year! For God's sake!!! She shouted. Just before she could say anymore, there was a gunshot that just went past her head. She crawled under the counter and made sure she was out of sight.

"Who the hell's in there!" Said a man who had just walked inside the shop. Eleanor put her hands out in the open and cried out.

"I am not a thief; I just didn't know where else to go, Mr. Farrow."

"Show yourself," he said grimly. Eleanor slowly got up from under the counter and stared at her attacker, whose face was not seen by the lack of light in the room. The attacker dropped his gun and stared blankly back at her. "Oh my sweet god, Ellie?"

"Yes?" she asked. The man walked slowly up to the lantern that was sitting on the counter. His facial features slowly formed into a familiar face; a face she could not believe she was seeing. "Jacob?" He nodded, and tears swelled in his eyes at the sight of her. The young man that once was Jacob Farrow was now much older, he had now grown a large bushy mustache, and his hair looked much thicker and unkept than it was when she saw him last. Jacob walked around the counter and stood right in front of Eleanor.

"I thought you were gone, girl," he said as he hugged her tighter than anybody had ever hugged someone. Eleanor grasped him tightly as well. She could not believe how old Jacob looked; he looked as though he was now in his twenties, even though she knew that by this point, he was barely nineteen. When they stopped hugging, Jacob looked deeply into Eleanor's eyes. "I knew you weren't dead; I just knew it!!!"

"Jacob, I'm okay," she said compassionately. Jacob began to break down in tears as he grasped her again. Eleanor held onto him as he wept into her jacket.

***

Jacob lit several more lanterns around the shop; the more he lit, the more the shop looked less and less familiar to her. New weapons and farming equipment were hanging off the walls of the main room. Eleanor did not notice this earlier, but there was a painting of Mr. Farrow on the right wall of the main room. He was holding a musket and wore a soldier's uniform. She looked at Jacob when he was done lighting the lanterns.

"Is your dad—"

"Yeah, passed last month, I'm afraid," Eleanor thought back to the last time she saw Mr. Farrow. He was so kind when he let them in the backroom and showed them the blade he was working on. He was one of the only people besides Jacob to stand up to Paster Please. "But I got the shop, and I've been workin' my tail off ever since then; it's good work."

"I'm glad you're happy, Jacob," she said with a half-assed smile. He pulled out a glass of rum from behind the counter and poured them both a glass and sat down in the middle of the room. There was an awkward silence in the room; neither of them knew where to start as far as questions go. "What did I miss?" Eleanor blurted. Jacob took a long sip of his rum and placed it by his chair.

"No, first you tell me where you were that night."

"Your birthday?"

"Yes, one minute you're telling me not to marry Eliza, and the second I go back to the party, you were gone. Then about five minutes later, Eliza told me that you had to go back home because you were sick," Jacob explained. Eleanor scoffed at that story as she took down her rum in one gulp.

"That's not what happened," as she pointed out that the rum bottle wanted a refill. Jacob kindly did so, as Eleanor explained. "She attacked me, stabbed me, and then threw me into a pond."

"WHAT!!!"

"She wanted to make sure that she had you all to herself and that I would not even think about being with you, so she took it upon herself to take me out of the picture."

"Oh my god, Ellie, I'm so sorry" Tears formed in Eleanor's eyes just by her retelling the story of her demise; she took another giant gulp of rum and poured herself another. "If it makes you feel any better, I'm not married."

"You're not?"

"Nope, I took your word for it, told my dad how I felt, and he and the pastor got to talkin', and that was that though believe me, Eliza's tried to get cordial with me, but I don't let her. I always knew something was wrong with her, and now I have living proof here!!!" Eleanor nodded in agreement. "But that still doesn't explain where you were for a whole year" Eleanor gave Jacob a grim look; silence spread through the shop like a thick smog.

"Okay, Jacob, what I am about to tell you sounds mad, but I want you to keep an open mind, okay?" Jacob nodded as well.

"I think I was dead for the majority of that time."

"What do you mean?"

"Jacob, I was dead, but something happened. I saw my funeral, and then I heard a voice saying, 'Not yet, you're not."

"Not yet?"

"And then I woke up, and I found this right next to where I washed up on the shore," Eleanor said just when she pulled out the book. She handed it to Jacob, who studied it carefully.

"What is it?" he asked. Eleanor grabbed the book again and replied.

"I don't exactly know but watch this" Eleanor cleared her throat and flipped to a familiar page in the book. "Gratis Lostrus" instantly, the book ignited with a bright blue light radiating from the pages. Jacob fell backward from his chair and spilled some of the rum next to it.

"Jesus Christ! What the hell did you just—" Eleanor closed the book, and the light that was inside slowly dimmed.

"Jacob, I think God brought me back because I have some unfinished business, I need to take care of."

"And what kind of business would you be implying?" Eleanor looked out the window and gazed upon the church. She took one final swig of rum from her glass as she said.

"Hell hath no fury as a woman scorned."

Chapter 4

The Wrath of Eleanor Shrowl

After Eleanor and Jacob's discussion, they decided it was best to go to bed. At that point, it was almost ten, and Eleanor felt as though she could pass out at any minute because of both exhaustion and alcohol. Jacob took her back to his house, which was connected to the shop. *No wonder he came in as quickly as he did,* she thought. The living room had no decorations on any of the walls. It was as bland as bland could get as far as a living arrangement went. Like with Delilah's cabin, there was a fireplace on the room's left side. Jacob went into one of the other rooms and came out with a pillow and quilt.

"Thank you," she said as she attempted to take both the quilt and the pillow from his hands.

"Oh, this isn't for you; you'll be in my room for the time being," he said generously.

"Oh, Jacob, I don't want to intrude. This is your home,"

"And now it's yours," he smiled. "You get some rest, okay?" Eleanor nodded her head and proceeded into Jacob's bedroom; she then climbed into her bed. Sleep did not come easy for Eleanor; she still thought much about Peter and her parents. *I'll see you soon,* she thought.

***

The next morning came quicker than Eleanor realized. It felt as though she had only slept for maybe three hours. She groggily got out of bed and lazily walked into the living room. She had thought she would see Jacob sleeping on one of the chairs next to the fireplace, but he was nowhere to be seen. Eleanor went back into her room and looked again at the book.

She flipped through several different pages, each of which had a mixture of gruesome drawings of people being hung, burned, and even skewered through the genitalia. Those pages always had some weird writing that Eleanor could never make out. It looked as though it was an old language, maybe even older than the original scripture of the bible. Several pages were written in English; each one of these incantations had a label telling the reader exactly what each one did. She had flipped to a page she had not been on before and found an incantation that intrigued her.

Confrigorgus- Conjure any item one thinks. (Does not work on summoning people)

"Any item?" she said to herself. She looked at the bed and imagined a large loaf of bread. She then uttered the words. "Confrigorgus" Instantly, a large loaf of bread appeared at the foot of the bed. She then grabbed it; it was warm to the touch. Eleanor took a huge bite out of it, and it was the best bread she had ever eaten, warm and soft. The only other thing that came close to being this good was when her grandmother would make pastries for her and Peter when she was still alive. She then heard the front door open and a familiar voice ring through the cabin.

"Jake? Are you here? I have today's orders for you; you'll never guess who needs more ammunition." Eleanor knew that voice though it sounded a slight octave lower than it usually did. *Could it be?* Eleanor opened the bedroom door and walked out of the bedroom, and the woman who had walked in was sitting by the fireplace. "Jake was someone here toni—" she said before she was cut off. Greta's eyes bulged at the sight of her once thought-dead friend standing in front of her, alive and well. Looking at how she was when she disappeared. Having not aged a day.

"Hi," Eleanor said nonchalantly. Greta stood there in shocked horror; she looked at Eleanor as if she was looking at her parents making love. Without a word, Greta fainted in one of the chairs next to the fireplace.

***

Several minutes passed after Greta fainted; Eleanor covered her forehead with a warm rag and placed the quilt that Jacob had covered himself with the night prior. *Way to go, Ellie,* she thought as she made sure her friend was in a more comfortable setting. Eleanor got a good look at her new, much older friend. Her hair was a darker shade of brown than it was before. She had horrible acne that had spread to her cheeks. Greta looked about a couple of inches taller than she was before. Before she fainted, Eleanor clearly remembered them looking at each other face to face; Greta was always a couple of inches shorter than Eleanor.

"Finally hit that growth spurt didn't help ya," she told herself as she rested. Eleanor thought that she was never going to see her friend again, and her hopes were high for her reunion with her family. Next to Greta were some documents that Eleanor assumed were for Jacob. She picked them up and looked them over. There was an order for ammunition made out to Pastor John Flease. "The bastard is still alive?" She looked through the other documents and found an order for a musket by a man named Donovan, along with several other orders for ammunition.

Out of nowhere, the front door flung open, and Jacob stood there with a handful of groceries. He smiled for about three seconds until she looked at the armchair next to the fireplace and saw Greta. Eleanor smiled slightly as he came closer.

"Did she—"

"Yeah..." Eleanor said awkwardly. They both looked at their friend empathetically and lovingly. Eleanor thought that this would have been what her parents felt like when either Peter or she fell asleep. Only in this case, it was poor Greta who took the shock of her friend's sudden reincarnation. Eleanor helped Jacob unload some of his groceries around the house. He had gotten more bread and butter, along with several pails of water from the large well in the middle of town. Jacob also grabbed several bags of sugar, spices, and veggies. Five minutes went by during this unpacking before both Eleanor and Jacob heard the chair

Greta was sitting on slowly creak as she stood up, delirious from her fainting spell.

"Hey Greta, are you okay?" Jacob said as he handed her a glass of water. Greta practically chugged the water when she was handed it.

"Yeah, I thought I saw Ellie aga—" she said before getting cut off at the sight of her friend. "Oh, my God! Oh my God! OH MY GOD!!!" Greta said excitedly as she jumped out from her seat and manhandled Eleanor. Tears started to form in Eleanor's eyes as she held her friend in her arms once again. Greta began to sob as well, her face became red, and her eyes were puffy from the tears. "I thought we lost you, El."

"I'm alright, Greta, I'm alright."

***

Both Jacob and Eleanor caught Greta up to speed about the events that unfolded. How Eliza 'killed' Eleanor and dumped her body in the pond, the vision that Eleanor had, as well as the book that she found as soon as she was out of the pond. All of this information enraged Greta as well as Jacob; his feelings from last night started bubbling up once again just by Eleanor retelling the tale of her demise.

"That crazy bitch!!!" Greta exclaimed. "I knew she had it out for you, but to think that she would try to kill you, that's insanity!!!" Jacob nodded his head in agreement with her statement. "All this time, we thought that you were killed by a bear or a wolf pack or something, but murder... It's sickening."

"Agreed, and let me tell you, it's not fun. I can't wait to see the look on Father's face when he sees me."

"Greta, she needs to know," Jacob muttered.

"Know what?" Eleanor asked. There was an awkward silence between the three of them. Greta clutched Eleanor's hand tightly.

"Ellie, your parents are gone,"

"WHAT!!!"

"After you disappeared, Please caught your mother on the job, you might say, with one of the farmers one night when he was on a walk. He had the whole town rallied together, and they drove them out. Nobody knows where they had gone; I'm so sorry, Ellie" Silence bared down on the room; it was like a shroud of deafening, heartbreaking, ear-ringing silence. Eleanor broke down on the floor and whimpered. Greta and Jacob both got down to their knees and comforted her the best they could. Eleanor felt a pain in her chest, a sharp pain much like the knife that Eliza used to cut through her flesh. The thought of her parent's departure was agonizing, more agonizing than her death.

"Why couldn't you help them," Eleanor asked both Greta and Jacob.

"El, if we did, our families would have had the same thing happen to them as well. We had no choice; we weren't a part of it; in fact, Greta tried her utter best to talk to Pastor Please and persuade him to change his mind, but—"

"But what?"

"That doesn't matter," Greta interrupted. "What does matter is that you are alive and well."

"NO—" Eleanor shouted as she got up and slowly walked to the window. "What matters now is what I'm going to do to Eliza and her bastard of a father for what they did to my family and me."

"Ellie, think abo—"

"What is there to think about Jacob? They tried to kill me, and they drove my family out of our town!!! I am not going to stand by and do nothing!!!" Eleanor shouted.

"I entirely agree, they need to answer for what they did, but we cannot butcher them as they tried with you; we need to be better than them. Promise me that you will not kill them." There was silence once again in the room. Everything in Eleanor's body wanted blood, wanted the sweet release of the Flease's being put down like the dogs they are. But she knew in her heart that she did not have the capacity for murder, no matter who it was.

"Yo-your right, we have to be better."

"So you promise not to kill them?" Greta asked.

"I promise,"

"So what exactly are we going to do?"

"The Flease's believed that my family was hell spawn, so let's give them hell," Eleanor said with an evil smile.

***

Eleanor immediately went into the next room and grabbed the book from Jacob's bedroom. She took into the main room and sat down in front of the fireplace. Eleanor flipped through it rigorously; both Jacob and Greta crowded around her when she did so. Both of them looked very curious about what exactly she was looking for in this mysterious book. She then stopped on one page, a familiar page. The page she was on just ten minutes ago. That page, along with several more behind it, had several lists of spells and incantations, all of which were labeled. Some of which were in black ink, some in red with what Eleanor hoped was ink. Eleanor looked up at both of them with that same smile she had before.

"This is how we get back on those damn Flease's." Jacob's eyes bulged at the thought of what Eleanor could do with what he saw last night with the book. Greta, on the other hand, looked slightly confused.

"An old book? How is that going to do anything?" Jacob and Eleanor both looked at her and smiled. Greta was now looking concerned as to why they were looking at her that way. "What?" she asked.

"Ellie show her," Jacob pressed. Eleanor stood up and walked to the center of the room. She looked around the room and smiled.

"Jacob, how do you feel about a little renovating?" she asked.

"What kind of renovations?" he asked cautiously. Eleanor flipped to the page with the conjuration spell and recited.

"CONFRIGORGUS!" a couple of seconds passed until candle pieces appeared from nowhere in the corners of the room. The small table that only sat one person in the kitchen suddenly stretched to fit seven. Just over the top of that newly stretched table was a chandelier that appeared with freshly lit candles. The wooden furniture that was in front of the fireplace suddenly turned into red cushioned seats, the kind you would see in Europe. The fireplace grew larger than it was before; not only did the size of the fireplace grow, but so did the fire itself. Several paintings of nature and various animals appeared around the room as well. There was a variety of different birds, deer, and several other animals, such as bears and squirrels, in these paintings. Around the main room as well as the area that was designated the kitchen, were vines that etched the top portion of the room, almost touching the ceiling. The vines slowly began to gestate several flowers with a variety of colors. The room itself felt as though it was glowing, not because of the natural light outside but because of the life that was being brought into it as well as the light the candles gave off around the room and from the fireplace. The last thing that appeared was several rugs that were placed under the new kitchen and several more around the house. The last of which was a black bear skin rug that appeared just in front of the fireplace.

Eleanor glanced around the room in awe of what she had created with just words and her thoughts. It was at this moment that she felt as though she could do anything; she felt as though God had blessed her with an incredible gift. *Is this what God felt like when he created the world in seven days?* She thought to herself the house was more beautiful than she could have imagined. Excitement and joy filled her bones as Eleanor cheered at the magik that she had just performed. She looked back at Greta and Jacob, who stood where they were and glanced around the house in shock and awe. Eleanor had never seen Greta so speechless in her life; she was more of a talkative person. But at this point, Eleanor could only assume that words could not describe what she had just witnessed.

"Oh my sweet God," Jacob muttered.

"What do you think? Do you like it?" Eleanor asked. "I know I should have talked about it more with you, but I mean, doesn't this feel more like a home than it did before?"

"It certainly does, El; this is incredible! " Jacob said as he hugged her tightly. In his arms, Eleanor was blushing harder than she ever did. She looked in front of her and saw Greta still standing, where she was still in shock. Eleanor stopped hugging Jacob and walked up to Greta.

"What do you think?"

"Ho-how?" she stuttered.

"I don't exactly know how, but this book can do anything," she said when she tried handing the book to her. Greta took a step away as she did so. "It's okay," Greta carefully took the book out of her hands and flipped through the pages.

"What are we going to do with this book?"

"Anything we want," Eleanor grinned.

***

Both Greta and Eleanor set out onto the town. Jacob could not join because he had to look after the shop. Outside, Eleanor made sure that her face was heavily covered; she did not want to be recognized amongst the townspeople who, for the most part, seemed brand new to Florence (or at least brand new to her). The day itself was cloudy and grim, but it gave Eleanor a better look at the buildings compared to when she first arrived. The schoolhouse looked to be much older. It had large vines etched across the left-hand side of it.

The large well that stood in the middle of town looked to be three sizes bigger than it was; the last time Eleanor saw the well, it had to be five feet in diameter. Now it looked as though it doubled. *The town probably expanded; that's why they needed a larger well,* she thought. She and Greta walked past several houses that she did not recognize. Many of them seemed to be double the size of Eleanor's house (or what was her house).

Out of nowhere, an old woman in her early forties stumbled onto her. Eleanor helped her up and got a good look; she couldn't believe her eyes; it was Sister Ingrid, but not in her typical attire but in old, ragged clothes, she had a large scratch just over her eyebrow, and her eyes looked puffy and red.

"Please, madam, could you spare me some food." Without hesitation, Eleanor looked at Greta, and they both walked her over to a stand they had seen earlier. Greta gave Eleanor some silver coins, and she bought the lady a large loaf of bread. Sister Ingrid scarfed down that bread as if she had a time limit for eating it. "Bless you, child, bless you," she said just before walking away. Eleanor looked at her from behind and thought back to all the classes she had had with Sister Ingrid. She was the one who taught Eleanor to read in the first place, and here she is now, a homeless, helpless woman who is just trying to survive.

"Greta, what happened to her?" Eleanor said, still looking at Sister Ingrid. Before Greta could answer, she was interrupted by a familiar voice. A voice Eleanor did not want to hear more than anything else in the world. The voice of her killer, walking free.

"WHAT DO YOU THINK YOU'RE DOING TOADSTOOL!!!" Both Greta and Eleanor jumped and turned around to see Eliza Flease, along with her other cronies, in the most elegant dresses Eleanor had ever seen. Eliza was wearing a poofy red dress and a burgundy corset that was so tight around her stomach and waist that it made her washboard chest look like she had large bosoms. Eliza walked up to Greta, pulled her white glove off, and slapped Greta across the face with it. "What have I told you about spending my money on them," she said disgustedly, looking at some of the townspeople. Greta looking furious looked back at her and said.

"They don't deserve it...."

"That's a good Toadstool." Eleanor looked at the face of her killer through her hood. She could feel the fire in her eyes as she gazed at Eliza. She clenched her fist so tightly that she felt her nails begin to dig into her skin. *You're going to pay for that,* she thought with her eyes glued to Eliza. Her body felt warmer the more she looked at her; it was like there was a fire brewing inside of her, ready to explode. Eliza looked at Eleanor and didn't catch her face.

"You there, shoo, I would have a word with this one here, and I would rather not catch whatever illness you possess, thank you" Her friends behind her giggled manically at that comment. Fighting every urge to beat on Eliza, Eleanor unclenched her fist and slowly walked back to the blacksmith's shop. She looked out the window again and saw Eliza speaking to Greta; she could not hear exactly what was going on between the two, but as soon as they were done talking, Greta was in tears as she walked back to the shop.

"What did she want?" Eleanor asked. Greta did not answer; she just sat down quietly on one of the new cushioned seats next to the fireplace. "Greta, what's going on?"

"About a month after you 'died', and your family was taken out of town Pastor Flease ran for the landlord; and won he and his family have been running the town thinking they're kings and royalty. They have bought so much land and resources they practically are royalty around her. The worst part is they have rich families and bankers from England backing up their finances. They come by and supply resources as well as have a few laughs at their new farmhouse just outside of town. Hell, Paster Flease has a giant vault in his new office where he keeps all the gold and silver he had shaken down from everyone in town. They took everything they could from these people, they started charging more for the blessings in church. Now people could barely afford food for themselves or their families. The Flease's gained their riches from both the town and the rich families that support them." Eleanor was stunned by this news. *As if that man needed more of a superiority complex,* she thought. "Ellie, I work for them along with the rest of the town. She asked me if I sent out the invitations to their next big gathering, which I did. She then threatened to fire me if she ever caught me with you or anyone else whom she deemed not worthy of her time."

"When's their next gathering?" Eleanor asked.

"Tonight at seven, why?" Without answering, Eleanor gave Greta an evil smile; Greta then put together what she was gathering and smiled back.

***

Greta and Eleanor spent the entire day planning the attack on the Flease's. They knew now that there was going to be a large party for them at their farmhouse; Eleanor made sure she knew exactly which house it was (though it was fairly obvious since it was the biggest in town). Not only did Eleanor double-check which house it was, but she combed through the book thoroughly; she had found pages that she had not peered on before, some of which had red and black pictures of goats surrounded by black smog. She stopped on one page that caught her eye; this page looked much like the page she usually read from; however, spells were inked in red ink instead of black. Not only that but there were no explanations as to what these spells did. Something about these spells did not seem right, but she pushed that thought back. Greta told her earlier not to test out any of the other spells; she didn't want to risk either of them getting hurt accidentally. Eleanor agreed; the only people she intended to hurt were the Flease's.

Eleanor looked back to the red-inked page and thought for a second. *Why would Morganna Starr not tell what these spells are? Perhaps they are too awful to be put into words.* She then thought about how Eliza treated Greta and how her parents must have felt when they were thrown out of town. Rage consumed her like fire; she felt her chest feel warmer the more she thought about it. She glared down upon the page, and without any more hesitation, she made up her mind.

Moments later, Jacob came in; it was half past six, and the sun was beginning to set.

"Jacob, we're going to ruin the Flease's party tonight," Eleanor said just as he shut the door behind him. Before she could explain the plan, any further Jacob cut her off.

"I was invited to the party."

"What? Jacob, you know what those people did to my family and me, right?"

"Yes, but I am not going for their benefit,"

"What do you mean?" Greta asked.

"I figured you two would like to have someone on the inside," Jacob explained. "If I'm there, I will be able to signal you two from inside when the appropriate time comes."

"Jacob, I don't think you want to be in there for what I am going to do to those people; not only that, but I don't want to see you get hurt."

"How about this? I will find another way out of the house when I give you the signal" Eleanor took a couple of seconds to think about this new plan Jacob had thought of.

"I don't know."

"Ellie, trust me, those Flease's have been nothing but cruel and heartless, and I want to help" Eleanor looked deeply into Jacob's blue eyes once again; she felt like she was drowning in the deep beautiful blue of his eyes.

"Okay but be careful."

"I will, plus I want to see the look on ole' man Flease when he sees his fancy party ruined."

"Agreed, but there is one thing we didn't consider," Greta added. "Ellie, does the book only work when you can see where you are casting?" Eleanor had not thought about that before. She thought back to the only times she did use the book, both of which she had to be directly looking at where she wanted to perform magik.

"I do not know; let's try it out." She grabbed a small candlestick from the kitchen and placed an unlit candle in it. Eleanor then placed it on the kitchen table. "I am going to try and light the candle from the other room. I need you both to tell me if it is lit or not, okay?

"Got it," they both said. Eleanor walked back into Jacob's bedroom and closed the door behind her. She then looked into the door and spoke the spell.

"Gratis Lostrus" A few seconds had gone by, and nothing had happened; she did not hear anything from the main room, nor did anything light up in Jacob's bedroom. Eleanor then tried thinking about the candle in the next room. She thought about the exact spot she had on the table and how the wick of the candle was positioned on the stem of wax it was on. "Gratis Lostrus," she spoke again. Just like last time, nothing. "Did the candlelight up?" she yelled to the next room.

"No," Greta yelled back. Eleanor then stepped out of the room and looked directly at the candle just from where she was standing. She concentrated hard on the exact placement of the candle once again and spoke.

"Gratis Lostrus" The second the words left her lips, the candle ignited almost instantly. Both Greta and Jacob were amazed just by the fact that she could light a candle from that distance and with words, no less. "Well, that answers that question. Now how do we use the book on the Flease's if we can't even get inside? I have been directly looking at where I want to cast" A few seconds went by, and Jacob snapped his fingers loudly. He then grabbed both Greta's and Eleanor's hands and walked them over to the front window.

"Look!" He pointed at a large hill that had a large, twisted oak tree that stood on the left side of the farmhouse. "That hill overlooks the main room where the party is. You two hide behind that tree and use the book from there!"

"Jacob, you're a genius!!!" Eleanor exclaimed. She then hugged him tightly and whispered in his ear. "Thank you"

"You're welcome; I got to get changed; I will be right back" Jacob rushed into his bedroom, leaving both Greta and Eleanor in the main room. Eleanor looked at Greta, who was smiling snidely.

"What?" Eleanor asked.

"Your face is red, hun," Greta said. Eleanor looked at her reflection from the window and saw that Greta was right. She was blushing hard. "You know you two are meant for each other, right?"

"What?" Eleanor said flabbergasted. "How could you—I mean—"

"You should talk to him, Ellie; tell him how you really feel." Eleanor looked back and forth between his room and Greta, contemplating what she wanted to do.

"I don't know Greta, I—"

"Look, when you—died—nobody was more devastated than your family and I but Jacob; he took it incredibly hard; there were nights I would have to help him home because he had drank so much. I mean, why do you think he lived alone all this time?" Eleanor had not considered this fact when she came back. Then again, she had a lot more on her mind at the time.

"I thought it was because of his father passing."

"It was not just his passing that shook him up; it started with yours and only got worse from there."

"Oh, poor man," Eleanor said while looking back at Jacob's room. "Greta, do you think he—" Before she could finish her sentence, Jacob came in wearing nice navy dress robes and white garb. Jacob went the extra mile and slicked back his long brown hair.

"How do I look?" he asked. Eleanor was awestruck at the sight of Jacob looking so clean and elegant. He looked as though he ran a country, or what Eleanor thought one in that position would look like. Eleanor was lost for words; he cleaned up so well.

"You look great, Jacob, doesn't he, Ellie?"

"Yeah—you look amazing."

"Thank you, this was my father's. I thought it might fit," he said while checking himself out.

"It's perfect; you ready?" Eleanor asked. Jacob looked at her and, with a sinister smile, said.

"Hell yeah"

***

The time had come; the plan was set, and Eleanor had never been more ready, more determined in her life up until now. The mere feeling of her determination and drive for revenge felt like sugar on her tongue. It was sweet and slightly bitter but in a good way. She had never felt this sort of way in her life. Sure, she had pulled a few jokes on her parents in the past, but this, this was something far, far worse than any sort of practical joke. On their way to the country house, Eleanor and Greta looked through the book frantically, looking for the perfect spells to use on Eliza and the rest of the rich pricks who were enjoying themselves at their little party. While they were looking, Eleanor noticed that Jacob was not with them. They had all left together around the same time; she looked behind her and saw him running back to the blacksmith's shop. Greta and Eleanor both stopped and waited for Jacob to return.

"What's he doing?" Greta asked.

"I do not know," Eleanor replied. A few seconds after she responds, Jacob comes rushing out of the shop with something wrapped around his arms. Eleanor could hear the clashing of metal as he made his way over. "What are you—" Eleanor said before realizing what he had. In Jacob's arms, wrapped very loosely were chains and large locks. She looked at Jacob with eyes of intent, and he gave her the same look. In that split second, Eleanor knew exactly what he was going to do.

"Jacob, you are brilliant!" Eleanor said in sheer excitement.

"I know," he replied both proudly and sarcastically. They then continued their venture to the Flease's country house. The village of Florence was now completely put to sleep, which is typical for this time of day. Most of the people in the village are farmers and craftsmen who tend to wake up an hour before the sun rises for their chores and other work they might do at that hour.

As they made their way through the town, Eleanor could see many lights from the houses, slowly dim. This made her remember how her father would get her into bed by this time, how he would recite Shakespeare and add his little flare to his recitals. If writing had not enticed her so much, Eleanor would have loved to be a player in a show of some kind. She had never seen any such shows, but she would love to at some point in time. The thought of her father, mother, and Peter being shunned out of town came like she was struck by lightning. And like most things, when lightning strikes it, the thing in question usually catches fire. And Eleanor was about to burst into flames and unleash her wraith upon those who wronged her.

The plan was slightly altered thanks to Jacob's last-minute decision-making. Instead, he was going to chain the doors of the country house and make sure everyone was inside by glancing in the windows discretely. They were about halfway to the house, and Greta was ahead of Jacob and Eleanor, who were still glancing through the book as if her life depended on it. Eleanor felt a warm hand on her shoulder; it was Jacob wrapping his jacket around her. She looked at him, confused but glad he did so. The wind was beginning to pick up, and it was difficult for Eleanor to keep the pages from flying through her fingertips.

"You seemed cold," Jacob said awkwardly.

"Thank you"

"It's no problem at all, Eleanor."

"No, thank you for everything," Eleanor closed the book and stopped walking altogether. "I know that what we are going to do is a big risk if either of you gets caught and if you both want to leave now. Now is your chance; you don't have to do this." Greta stopped; there was a momentary silence that was quickly broken by the sound of Greta walking towards Eleanor with vigor in her step.

"You must be having a laugh if you think that I don't want to see those damn Flease's pay for what they have done to us and the town. Not to mention what they did to you and your family. Ellie, I want to see them suffer as much as you and the rest of the townspeople here suffer under their reign." Greta said with hatred and determination.

"Damn right, they hurt you more than anybody could; Eleanor and I would love more than anything to see them feel that same level of torment they put you, your family, and the townspeople here," Jacob added.

"You both never mentioned what they did to the townspeople... what did they do to them?" Eleanor asked. There was silence again, and Jacob and Greta locked eyes for a couple of seconds. Eleanor saw this and knew they were holding something back. "What did they do to them, guys?"

"The Flease's have enforced a tax that has nearly crippled everyone who lives in Florence; the only ones who are barely able to feed their families are those who work for them like myself and Jacob. We try to give as much as we can, but if we were ever caught being generous to the less fortunate. Or, in other words, those that don't work for the Flease's, we'd be—"

"Shunned as well," Eleanor finished her sentence. "That's why you were hesitant about helping out Sister today because you were worried about getting caught by the Flease's."

"Which I was and given one final chance at redemption, one more 'betrayal of their wealth,' and I will be tossed out of Florence as well."

"But what about those who do not work for the Flease's? What happens to them?" Eleanor asked.

"They are left to fend for themselves," Jacob muttered. Eleanor looked upon both of them in horror. Rage started to fill her bones and muscles like hot air. She then grabbed Jacob by the hand and proceeded to march along to the country house. If there was any shred of doubt in her actions before, it was gone now. *This is not just for me; this is for Greta, for Jacob, and for Florence!!!* She thought as they reached the country house minutes later.

The house itself was grand; it was two stories tall, and the wood looked lacquered as if each board made into this house had to be polished to perfection. The front door was massive and looked like it was made of marble, even though Eleanor knew it couldn't be. There was a large chimney in the middle of the roof with smoke coming from it. Guaranteed, the Flease's have a large fire made in the middle of the house. Unlike most houses Eleanor had seen before, this one, in particular, was much wider; it was as if this house had broad shoulders. She thought of the kind of broad shoulders one might see on a wood chopper or a blacksmith like Jacob. She pushed that thought behind, and she and Greta made their way to the eastern part of the house, where they said they would be able to see the party. The tree that stood at the top of the hillside was twisted and crooked. The tree's main trunk looked as though it was made out of the thickest rope Eleanor had ever seen. She had never seen this tree before; the branches had no leaves on them but stretched in every direction.

When they got to the top of the hill, Eleanor and Greta made sure to crouch behind the tree so that their light would not be seen by the people in the house. Eleanor glanced around and saw the large window that Greta and Jacob were talking about, and they were not kidding when they said that the window was large enough for her to see. The window stretched from the base of the house to the second floor. Eleanor had a clear view of the party that was going on downstairs. The fireplace that stood in the middle of the house was the largest she had ever seen before; Hanging over top of the fireplace was the paster holy silver blade, along with several bookcases and an adjoining kitchen area and study. *The bedrooms are most likely upstairs. But why would they put such a large window right here? Of all places?* Eleanor looked around, and behind the tree and the hill was a large lake with a large cluster of trees behind it; she looked back at the window and the lake. *The view* she realized. She could not tell how good this view was because of how dark it was, but if it was enough for the Flease's to build that into their house clearly, it must be some sight to see.

Inside, the party had amassed over thirty people, all of whom were wearing their best dress clothes and gowns. In the middle of the living room were ten people holding hands and moving in a circle; in the middle was Eliza with a blindfold on. She was wearing a pear-green dress that made the bottom half of her look like a cloud. From what Eleanor could gather, they were playing blind man's bluff. If there were a better time to commence with the plan, now would be the time. A few seconds after she and Greta looked into the house, Jacob came running back to the tree.

"Doors are now officially locked; what do you suppose we do first?" he asked. Eleanor looked in the book and found a perfect spell to use on Eliza because she was blindfolded and an easy target. Eleanor peered over the tree into the house once again, and in front of the fireplace just behind Eliza was a coffee table with a fruit plate on it. Eleanor concentrated hard on the plate and where she wanted it to go. She imagined one of the large granny smith apples pelting Eliza in the head. Eleanor imagined it getting chucked so hard that the apple splattered everywhere. When she had that vivid image in her head, she went ahead and spoke the incantation.

"Kamarro" instantly hurled one of the fruit bowl apples directly into Eliza's face. When it struck her, Eliza hit the floor hard. The people around her looked awestruck and confused. Eleanor, Jacob, and Greta collectively burst into laughter. Eleanor had not laughed so hard; nothing was funnier than seeing Eliza getting pelted by a floating apple to the face. She tried to shush both Greta and Jacob so that the people inside could not hear them. Inside, everyone was looking around, trying to make heads or tails about how Eliza was struck. Paster Flease looked red in the face; from what Eleanor could gather, he had thought someone inside had thrown that apple at her. He had picked up Eliza, whose nose was now bleeding. *My God, I broke her nose!!!*

Eleanor realized. She had removed the blindfold and was crying in her father's arms. "Let's see how the paster feels about Melon, shall we?" Eleanor asked both Jacob and Greta. Just like last time, Eleanor concentrated again, putting a clear picture of what she wanted in her mind and speaking again. "Kamarro," just like Eliza, a large cantaloupe melon from the fruit bowl was hurled at Paster Flease's head. It struck him in the back of the head; once again, everyone inside looked shocked and confused by what had just happened. Without a moment to react, Eleanor repeated the incantation repeatedly.

"Kamarro, Kamarro, Kamarro!!!" Left and right random objects around the living room were being thrown at other party guests. Eleanor used the spell on chairs and books on the bookcases near the fireplace. Pots and pans from the kitchen crashed into people as they collectively tried to get out of the house. Eliza sadly was at the back of the pack of people trying to leave. Eleanor stared at her and recited a new spell she had never tried before. "Weivelo beru" Instantly, Eliza began to levitate off the ground. In Eleanor's ear, she heard Greta speak.

"Oh my God," Greta and Jacob were too stunned to speak. Eliza was floating in midair. Everyone at the party stopped trying to pry the doors open and stared at Eliza in horror. Eliza was hysterically screaming; she did not know what was going on or how she was floating. Paster Flease grabbed Eliza's torso to try and pull her back down, several other men tried doing the same, but nothing was working. Eleanor looked back in the book and saw next to the levitation spell, there was a drawing of a hand palm side up with arrows pointing up and down.

"I wonder," Eleanor spoke to herself. She rotated her hand into the position the page instructed and raised it slowly.

"Look!" Jacob said, pointing at the party. Eliza was slowly rising higher off the floor. Eleanor raised her hand higher and higher. Eliza's screams could be heard over everyone else's screams inside. The six men, along with Paster Flease, who was trying to pull her down, were now getting lifted with Eliza until a few seconds later when they all came crashing down onto the floor with the bottom half of Eliza's dress. Eleanor and Greta's eyes bulged, not because of her dress getting ripped in half but because Eliza was not wearing any sort of undergarments underneath. Greta immediately covered Jacob's eyes while also laughing once again at Eliza's situation.

"Is she—?" he asked, confused and dumbfounded. Greta, who was still looking at the party, nodded her head. Eleanor was more amazed than both of them. She did not plan on her dress ripping as it did; the fact that it did was hilarious on its own. She wasn't surprised to see that she was not wearing anything underneath. Eleanor thought back to the night she was killed and remembered Eliza dancing topless around the fire at Jacob's gathering. *Does this bitch own any sort of undergarments? She will come after tonight; that is a fact.* Eleanor raised her hand as high as possible until Eliza was six feet off the ground. She looked back at Greta and Jacob and smiled menacingly.

"And now for the finale!!!" Eleanor said excitedly. Once again, she concentrated not on one particular person but on everyone inside the party; once she had that clear image in her mind, she recited from the book again.

"Weivelo beru!!!" Just like Eliza, everyone started floating off the ground. Several of the men tried holding on to the furniture to try and ground themselves, but it did not work. The women cupped their hands at the front ends of their dresses so that they would not be turned inside out. Everyone inside was screaming their heads off, trying to wiggle around the room to try and get themselves back on the ground, but it was no use; they, much like Eliza, were suspended in mid-air. Eleanor looked back into the book once again and recited another spell. "NECRIUS!!!" she shouts. Instantly storm clouds start to form inside the house. The black and grey storm clouds begin to push the floating guests with a violent wind. Everyone inside was now twirled around like a ragdoll. The wind was picking up inside the house, and the clouds produced rain and lightning that showered everybody. The screams were almost completely masked by the pounding of thunder that was echoing throughout the house and could be heard outside. Eleanor could see that not only were the people floating being hurled around the house, but so was the furniture as well. The kitchen table, the chairs, and the books that were so neatly placed on the shelves were now being cycloned along with everything else inside the house.

Outside, Greta and Jacob were looking in the house, completely amazed by how much chaos Eleanor had created. Their laughs turned into looks of awe and astoundment. Eleanor felt a small tap on her shoulder from Jacob.

"I think that's enough for now, Ellie," he said, satisfied by what they had done.

"One more spell," she begged. Jacob nodded and let Eleanor read from the book one last time for the night. She found a spell she had not seen before but wanted to use. "Amplofi" She looked around and did not see anything happen. Nothing caught fire, and nothing moved around them. She looked at Greta and Jacob, and both of them shrugged their shoulders. Eleanor looked back in the book and read what the spell does.

Amplofi – amplify voice into any given space.

"Oh," Eleanor said in realization; a second after she said that she heard more screaming coming from inside. Eleanor looked at Jacob and Greta again, confused. She then spoke again. "OOOOOHHHH"

"Ellie, they can hear you!!!" Greta said, both frightened and amazed. Eleanor realized anything she said right now was now being projected inside the house. She thought extremely hard about what she would say, she did not want Eliza to know that she was alive. *So let's make it sound like I'm not alive,* she thought.

"E—LIZ—A FLEA—SEEE," Eleanor spoke in a spooky voice. Greta and Jacob were both giggling as she spoke more. "I HAVE RETURNED FROM THE GRAVE YOU PUT ME IN!!!" More screaming followed inside as the guests were still getting twirled around. Eleanor heard several people inside asking, 'Who said that?' and 'What do you want?' Eleanor spoke one last time. "I WILL HAVE MY REVENGE ELIZA SO SAYS THE SHROWL WITCH!!!" The screaming had now reached an all-time high, and everyone was spinning faster and faster around the room to the point they were reduced to a blur. Eleanor then pointed to the front door that Jacob had locked, signaling him to unlock the door. Eleanor still had her hands raised and was twirling them as the people inside moved just as fast as her hands. Jacob rushed down, removed the chains around the doors, and rushed back up to the tree. He then tapped Eleanor on the shoulder to show he had done so. Eleanor then muttered one final spell to end this sweet night of revenge and many more nights like this in the future. "UNDOS" Eleanor then whipped her hands in the direction the now unlocked doors were, and everyone, including Eliza and Paster Flease and the furniture that was flying, was shot out of the house and into the muddy trail. As soon as everyone was out of the house, Greta killed her lamp, and the trio began to pack up and head back to Jacob's house. Outside, everyone who was at the party was still screaming their heads off; some of the men and a few women threw up as they hit the ground. Eleanor must have spun them around so much that they lost their dinner. Nearly all of them either ran away from the house, returned to their carriages, and rode off into the night, never to be seen again. Eliza and her father were the only other people outside the house. Paster Flease was on his knees praying; Eleanor did not know exactly why he was doing that. Her best guess is that the man had been so scared that he thought praying might make him feel better. On the other hand, Eliza was covered in mud; the bottom half of her dress was still missing, and she was down on her knees, shaking. She did not move from that spot for half a minute until she eventually fainted. Paster Flease saw this and carried his daughter away from the house.

"Come on, let's move!!!" Jacob whispered. The trio made their way off the hill and decided to go through the woods around the town to get back to Jacob's house. Eleanor could see faintly through the trees where the paster was taking Eliza. It looked as though he was taking her to the church. *Does he think he'll be safe there? Not for long,* Eleanor thought. She decided she would wait for another time to torment the poster; right now, her only goal was to get to Jacob's house and not be caught doing it. Eleanor, Jacob, and Greta were now sprinting back to the house, and they reached it in less time than it took to get to Eliza's house. They made their way into the house from the back door and huddled in the living room, which was now pitch black.

"Gratis Lostrus," Eleanor spoke, and just like last time, all the candles in the room suddenly lit, and the room was now visible. Every one of them was huffing and out of breath they had run so hard and so fast, but Eleanor was positive that nobody spotted them. "We made it!!!" Eleanor shouted in excitement. Greta and Jacob both cheered with her. Eleanor had never felt this level of triumph in her life; it was like accomplishing a lifelong goal. Though then again, she had only just come back to life a few days ago. Without a moment's hesitation, Eleanor grabbed one of the standing candles near the doorframe and concentrated hard once again. "Cathratro" As she spoke, the standing candle turned into a large bottle of red wine and three glasses that had gold rims at the top and bottom.

"Hell, yes!!!" Jacob spoke as he rushed over to Eleanor to pop the cork of the wine glass. Greta came over as well, and Eleanor handed her a glass while Jacob poured them half a glass each. "A toast to--?" Jacob hesitated.

"The fall of the Fleases!!!" Greta shouted in triumph. The trio toasted to and drank their wine heavily.

***

The three of them drank for hours. Eleanor had conjured five bottles of wine out of several other things around the room that she had created earlier that day. It was now almost three a clock, and the only other light source that was in Jacob's house was that of the blazing fireplace in the living room. Greta had completely passed out on the couch. Jacob and Eleanor collectively did not drink nearly enough as Greta did. She seemed to be more overjoyed by the Flease's demise than Eleanor was. Halfway into their celebration, Greta had ditched using her glass and instead had Eleanor conjure the other three bottles just for her. If she had to guess, Eleanor would say that she and Jacob both drank just a single bottle for themselves. Eleanor and Jacob were both tired and very intoxicated. Jacob stumbled to the far-left corner of the room beside the fireplace, where he had a quilt rack set up. He pulled one of the quilts from it and covered Greta with it. He then grabbed another quilt and set it on the rocking chair that he had slept in the night prior.

"Are you going to sleep in here again?" Eleanor asked.

"Well, yes, do you want to sleep there?" Jacob responded. Eleanor didn't know how to respond. Her heart was beating faster than it ever was at that moment. She felt a spark both in her chest and her loins the more she inched closer and closer to Jacob. Her skin began to feel hot and tingly; she could not help it for what she was about to do. Eleanor placed her arms around Jacob and kissed him gently. His breath smelt of the wine they had both drank which had the scent of cherries and grapes with a hint of melon. The tingling sensation she was feeling intensified through her arms moved to her legs. Eleanor quickly stopped kissing Jacob and took a step back.

"I'm sorry I—" she said before she was caught off by Jacob pulling her back into his arms and kissing her back. This time Eleanor could not only feel his lips piercing hers, but she also felt his tongue slightly. With that sensation, Eleanor slipped her tongue into Jacob's. Both of which were in a sort of dance. Jacob, without breaking contact with Eleanor, picked her up just under the waist and was now holding her. Eleanor then wrapped her legs around Jacob as he began to carefully walk back into the bedroom, still holding Eleanor in his hulkish hands. Once inside, Jacob carefully placed Eleanor on his bed and began kissing down her face and her neck. Eleanor could not help but let out a slight squeal at the erotic sensations she was feeling all over her body. At the same time, he continued kissing Eleanor's neck and chest. Eleanor quickly undid the buttons on her blouse, which caught Jacob off guard.

"Are you—" Jacob muttered before he was cut off.

"Shut up and keep going" Eleanor and Jacob were now both taking their clothes off and exposing themselves to each other for the very first time. Jacob continued to kiss Eleanor's body as he continued further and further down. Eleanor had never felt anyone caress her body in such a way. She had never felt the sensation of someone sucking on her breasts as a child would on their mother. She did not want this sensation to stop; she wanted more. And Jacob gave her exactly that. Eleanor and Jacob made love for the rest of the night. By the time they were done, Eleanor and

Jacob were so exhausted they instantly fell asleep in Jacob's bed.

***

The sun gently shined into Eleanor's dreary eyes from the window. As she slowly began to wake herself up, her head started to ache as if an anvil had fallen upon it. *So this is what the morning sickness feels like,* she thought to herself. This was Eleanor's first official hangover; she only felt anything to this degree when she burst out of the salt-watered pond. She peered at herself under the sheets and saw that she was completely naked, along with Jacob, who was still sleeping. Her eyes bulged when she caught a glimpse of Jacob's flaccid penis that was drooping onto the mattress like a limp sausage. Eleanor looked at how the rest of the bed looked and saw that her clothes were scattered not only on the bed but also on the floor around it as well.

"Oh my god," she said softly. *Did Jacob and I have—"* The memory of Eleanor drunkenly kissing Jacob and being whisked off her feet into her room immediately reappeared in her mind. A large part of her felt as though she was going to leap in the air because of how happy she was to have finally expressed how she felt about Jacob. A small, small part of her felt a little guilty about taking advantage of how they were that night. Then again, they did have a lot to drink. *Not nearly enough as Greta—* "Oh my god Greta!" she said in realization. Once she had said that she felt Jacob roll over slightly on the mattress; the sun that had awoken, Eleanor flashed directly into his eyes. Eleanor looked at Jacob once again; she looked at him in a way a mother looked upon the children she had loved with every fiber of her heart. She gently leaned back again and began running her fingers through his hair. His thick dark brown hair felt as smooth as silk. Eleanor could tell that Jacob was enjoying the feeling of her fingers through his hair by how she groaned in soothing comfort. His eyes opened slowly and were met by Eleanor's.

"Morning," she said gently.

"Morning, Ellie," he said in response. He then pulled Eleanor closer to him just as he did last night and held her in his large arms. Eleanor could feel both her bare body and his getting hotter and hotter the longer they cuddled together. "This is nice," he said abruptly.

"Agreed" Eleanor did not want this moment to end if she wanted to; she could lie naked with Jacob till the end of time. "Don't ever let go," she said before kissing his large arms.

"Never, Ellie. Never" he said proudly. Eleanor slowly graced her hand across his cheek and kissed him, not as hard as last night and with no use of the tongue. But as gentle and soothing as she could ever be. Jacob kissed her back and smiled the biggest smile Eleanor had ever seen. She had never felt this much passion and longing for someone in her life. Eleanor gazed into his eyes as if they were the rarest jewels one could find.

"I adore you, Jacob Farrow," Eleanor said.

"And I, you Eleanor Shr—" A woman's screaming outside cut off his sentence, which made both Jacob and Eleanor jump slightly. The screaming continued as Jacob and Eleanor quickly got their clothes back on. They both raced out of the room and into the living room, where Greta was staring outside.

"Greta, what is it? What happened?" Eleanor asked hysterically as she approached the window. This was one of the only times Eleanor Shrowl was cut speechless by what she had seen outside. In the town square were several people whose skin had turned a bright yellow and were vomiting blood. A few of them were passed out on the ground, and Eleanor immediately knew they were dead. One of the bodies was of a little boy whose mother held him in her arms as she balled her eyes out and screamed in hysteria. Those that weren't dead or throwing up blood were at the well in the middle of town at the well where in the bucket, she had seen a large man pull out a dead cat drenched in water.

"OUR WATER HAD BEEN POISONED!!!" he shouted. Eleanor gazed outside in horror. She could not believe what she was seeing. *No, I could not have caused this!!! Could I?* She thought to herself. Eleanor, Jacob, and Greta all heard the church bell chime. In the town square stood Paster Flease screaming at the top of his lungs.

"THE DEVIL HAS COME TO FLORENCE!!! THE DEVIL HAS COME TO FLORENCE!!! INTO THE CHURCH!!! EVERYONE INTO THE CHURCH NOW!!!! Eleanor did not want to watch; she turned her back away from the window and was suddenly alone in Jacob's house. Both Greta and Jacob had both vanished. She looked left and right, and behind her, the window she had just looked through was now gone. When she turned around again, she was face to face with a young boy in odd clothing. He had black hair that looked to be standing on end. His clothing looked to be some sort of felt she did not recognize it. The boy looked at her with fear; it was as if he was looking at the face of a monster. When she inched her hand closer to him,

Eleanor saw in the corner of her eye that her hand was not as smooth as it was before. It looked as though it were made of leather, old brown leather that had been laid to rot for decades. She then looked at her other hand and saw that she could see her skeletal fingers. Her heart pounded like a drum faster and faster. Eleanor then let out the most bloodcurdling scream she had ever screamed in her life. The boy then screamed; he screamed until he was woken up by his mother.

Chapter 5

Verticus Klatos Delifushstro

Eleanor was lost for words at what she was seeing. From the window, she saw the children of Florence being carried out of their homes. Their eyes, nose, and mouths all have dried blood coming from them. Eleanor could hear the hallowed cries of mothers in every direction. She did not know what to make of it. Eleanor quickly went back into the room to put on some more clothing, it had all happened so fast that she did not have time to even put on a blouse. Jacob followed suit along with her.

"What the hell is happening?" Jacob asked hysterically.

"I don't know" she responded. Eleanor's mind was scattered in every direction. What could cause something like this? Eleanor saw how the town was yesterday, she remembered seeing children playing with a ball when she and Greta set out onto the town. She remembered that was one of the only good things she saw of her once beautiful village that had now turned sour by the stink of the Flease's. This was not what she expected the day to turn out. Eleanor was expecting the Flease's would be scared off by what she had done to them at their party. Part of her imagined how they would have looked when they were packing their belongings and leaving Florence for good. That would have been one of the best days Eleanor could have possibly imagined (besides last night when she used the book on Eliza and her party). More screams and wails followed as the town erupted more into chaos. It was at this point that Greta was finally awakened from her drunken slumber. Eleanor had completely forgotten that she had passed out last night.

"What's going on?" she said drowsily. Eleanor could not speak she was so confused by what was going on. Instead of answering her she just waved for her to come to the window where she was carefully looking outside without trying to be seen by the other townspeople. Just like Eleanor, when she saw what was going on she too gasped in shock as well. "What the bloody hell is going on?" she asked.

"I don't know," Eleanor replied. Just as she spoke louder screams bellowed into Jacob's house. Eleanor, Greta, and Jacob rushed to the other window on the left-hand side of the house and looked out at a woman in the middle of the town square where the watering well was. She had pulled out a bucket and dumped out what was inside. Inside the bucket was the severed head of a goat, as well as bloodstained water that covered the ground before it. Screaming was now coming from almost every direction at the sight of the severed goat head. Many of the farmers and the women gagged and threw up at the sight of it. Upon looking at this severed head Jacob clutched Eleanor in his arms and covered her eyes, so she did not have to watch. Whereas Greta immediately threw up her drinks from last night onto the floor.

"The water has been contaminated!!!!" said one of the villagers in the distance. Then a familiar voice is heard over all of the screaming and chaos of what has transpired.

"THE DEVIL HAS COME TO FLORENCE!!!" shouted Paster Flease. Everyone in the square had now become silent. The Pastor was accompanied by Eliza and her friends as well as several other town officials who were at the party last night.

"TIS TRUE THE DEVIL ATTACKED ME IN MY OWN HOME!!!" shouted Eliza. The townspeople now looked upon her with both horror and disbelief. "SOMEONE HERE HAD AWAKENED AN EVIL IN THIS TOWN AND IT HAS COME FOR OUR CHILDREN!!!" She added. Tired of hearing the Flease's speak Jacob walks outside being careful not to draw attention to Eleanor and Greta who stayed behind. All eyes were on Jacob as he walked out. Eliza rushes to Jacob expecting to be held in his arms, he immediately walks past her and shrugs her off. Jacob looks out into the crowd as he is now the center of attention.

"Are you all hearing this nonsense?" Jacob asked the crowd. There was a small silence, Eleanor and Greta watched as Jacob said his piece. "Children are dead, and you think it is because of the devil himself? It's obvious what has happened here"

"Then tell us!!!" yelled one of the farmers in the crowd. The rest of the crowd followed suit.

"Yes, tell us, blacksmith," said Pastor Flease condescendingly. Jacob walked over to where the goat's head was and gagged slightly.

"Someone has contaminated our water and our children; may they rest in peace got sick and that is the reason why they are dead!!!" Silence ensued the crowd again. It was a logical explanation of what was going on, everyone could see that could have been the case.

"That is some story, but answer us this boy, we all drink from that water how come we are not as dead as those children." Pastor Flease said while pointing at the row of dead children who have now been covered in tarps. The crowd then got riled up once again, that was the one flaw in Jacob's story.

"Oh no..." Eleanor spoke to herself. Jacob remained silent for a couple of seconds and spoke once again.

"How dare you!" Jacob exclaimed to the Pastor. "How dare you speak of our dead in that way! They were children of the lord, our lord! A lord that you of all people should believe in!" Without hesitation, Pastor Flease slaps Jacob across the face with his glove.

"YOU DARE QUESTION MY FAITH!!!"

"YES, I DARE BECAUSE YOU ARE SAYING THAT THE DEVIL HAS COME TO FLORENCE!!! WHAT KIND OF PRIEST WOULD LET THE POWER OF SATAN OVERWHELM HIS FAITH IN OUR FATHER GOD!!!" The gravity of Jacob's words hit home with everyone in the square as well as Greta and Eleanor. The silence that followed was somehow deafening to everyone at the moment. Jacob finally spoke again with tears in his eyes. "Our children are dead... we must bury them properly. We as a community must mourn and come together to find the culprit behind this crime" he said while holding the head of the goat for everyone to see. "Justice must be served, in the name of our children." With that final statement, the crowd finally dispersed. Pastor Flease and Eliza both gave Jacob a scowl as they too marched away from the well and into the church. Jacob then dropped the goat head and went back into his hut where Eleanor and Greta met with him. On the table was one of the last bottles of wine they had last night, it looked to be half full, Eleanor went over to the table and chugged the wine bottle until it was empty.

"Ellie, are you okay?" Jacob asked. She immediately shook her head no.

"By God what have I done..." there was silence in the room when she spoke. "Those kids are dead because of me, I released evil into Florence..."

***

"Ellie you can't possibly believe that the book is the reason those kids got sick," Greta asked.

"Greta those kids are now dead..." Eleanor replied. There was a small silence in the room. "You and I both know that those kids were perfectly fine yesterday and ever since we used the book not only are the kids dead but also our water is contaminated."

"Uhm Ellie" Jacob muttered.

"If we had not used the book not only would the town have a good water source but also those kids would be ALIVE!!!" Eleanor shouted.

"Ellie" Jacob repeated.

"Ellie the spells we used were against Eliza and the people at her party how could you think that could have affected the whole town?" Greta questioned.

"THE BOOK ITSELF IS EVIL WE ONLY USED IT FOR OURSELVES. AND BECAUSE OF THAT NOT ONLY DID WE EXPOSE OURSELVES TO THAT EVIL BUT WE EXPOSED THAT EVIL TO THE TOWN AND NOW KIDS ARE DEAD AND IT'S OUR FAULT!!!"

"ELEANOR SHROWL!!!" Jacob shouted.

"WHAT?" Eleanor replied as she walked over to him. Greta followed her and gasped at what she saw. On the counter in the kitchen area was a bowl of fruit that was now rotting. It looked as though it had been rotting for almost a year. Eleanor picked up an apple and it oozed into her hand. It let out a putrid smell as she held it, which caused her to gag.

"That's not all" Jacob added. He walked over to the back window overlooking the Red's farm. The cattle were now slumped over covered in flies. Xavier Red and his son Gregory Red were now checking the cattle which were dead with even Eleanor and Greta's eyes.

"Still think I'm mad?" Eleanor asked Greta. She remained silent.

***

Eleanor marched back to Jacob's bedroom where she had placed the book. She brought it into the living room for all of them to see. Eleanor was flipping through the pages frantically.

"Ellie, what are you doing?" Jacob asked. She did not answer, she continued to flip through the pages just as she had done before. Greta pulled her away from the book and looked her dead in the eyes.

"Ellie, what are you doing?" she asked as calmly as she could. Eleanor's eyes were now glassy, almost filled with tears.

"There's got to be a way I can reverse this, take back the magik we did, and save those kids."

"Ellie..." Greta said gingerly.

"NO!!! There has to be a way. There has to be something in this damn book that can save those kids!!!"

"Ellie, those kids are gone" Jacob added.

"Do not say that I can do it I can bring them back!" Eleanor pleaded.

"Ellie, they are gone..." Jacob said coldly. With that being said silence filled the room once more this time those words struck Eleanor straight to her heart. She did not want it to be true, and at that moment she finally broke down into tears, she wailed just as much as the mothers of those poor children who had perished by the evil that Eleanor had unleashed. Eleanor had collapsed in her sorrow and Jacob kindly carried her back into the bedroom and placed her in bed. Where he laid there with her into her tears of sorrow seized and she rested in an unpleasant sleep.

***

Eleanor awoke in a poorly lit room. Jacob's room was now only lit by a couple of candles. But these candles were different than the ones he had. The candles that illuminated the room were tall and the wax was black, whereas Jacob's were burgundy. Eleanor still had on the one piece of clothing she wore when she woke up earlier. She got up and got fully dressed. *Did I sleep all day?* She questioned, though the answer seemed clear she had. Jacob's room is a room where natural light overwhelms the room more than unnatural light. Eleanor opened the door thinking that there would be more light coming from the main room but there was none. The hallway leading from Jacob's room to the shop in the front was pitch dark. Eleanor grabbed one of the black candles that was by her bed and went out into the hallway. As she walked out, she couldn't help but notice the silence that was present. Eleanor's ears were slightly ringing due to how silent the hall was. Not only that but the hallway felt longer than it usually was. The only other thing that Eleanor could see through this darkness was a slight outline of the front door. Or what she hopes is the front door. As she walked, she felt uneasy, something was wrong and Eleanor knew it.

"Hello?" she asked into the darkness, hoping for a response. The only response she got was a more deafening silence. "Is there anyone here?" Eleanor asked again. Eleanor then heard a small splashing sound coming from behind her. She turned around and saw that the hallway that she had just walked down wasn't a hallway at all. Eleanor held the candle up to the ground and instead of seeing Jacob's wooden floors, it was now cold damp rock. She looked behind her once again and saw that the outlined door was still there, yet something told her that was not the door to Jacob's shop. She then heard the splashing sound again from where she walked. Eleanor looked in the direction the splashing was coming from.

"Hello? Is someone there?" she asked again. The only response that she received was the sound of more splashing it sounded as if the person she asked was now running directly to her. Without question, Eleanor ran away from the sound towards the doorway out of the cave. She did not know what this thing was that she was running from but that didn't matter now, what did matter was that she got out of wherever the hell she was in. As she ran closer and closer to the door she could feel that whatever was chasing her was closer than she thought. She was so scared that she did not dare to look behind her to see what was chasing her. When she finally reached the door, she opened it and slammed it shut behind her. This door that she had just walked through looked familiar. It was a red door with gold stars painted all over it—

"NOOOO!!!!" a woman shouted. Eleanor quickly turned around and realized where she was. She had thought she was in someone's house but instead, she was at the Pastor's mansion where she and Jacob and Greta used the book on Eliza. The entire town was here, almost everyone had torches and pitchforks with them. "PLEASE NO!!!" she heard again. Eleanor saw who the voice belonged to; her heart sank when she saw the terrified look on Greta's face as she was being dragged by her thrashing arms to Pastor Flease.

"GRETA TODDLE YOU ARE ACCUSED OF WITCHCRAFT, HOW DO YOU PLEA?"

"Burn in hell you vile—" Greta responded before Paster Flease slapped her across the face with his glove.

"SILENCE WITCH!!!" Everyone in the crowd started to get riled up as this went on. Eleanor did not know what to do other than just stand there and watch. "CONFESS!!! CONFESS THAT YOU USED WITCHCRAFT AND BROUGHT UPON THIS DARKNESS INTO OUR TOWN!!!" Greta remained silent; she did not want to look at him. Eleanor got up close and saw that nobody else could see her, including Greta and the Pastor. Eleanor was now right up in Greta's teary-eyed dirt-covered face. She was shaking, shaking so horribly out of fear of what would happen. Disappointed that she did not answer the Pastor looked over to Eliza and asked. "What should we do to this pawn of evil darling?" Eliza gazed upon Greta who then looked up to her with tears strolling from her eyes. Eleanor saw Eliza give the most menacing smile she had ever seen.

"BURN THE WITCH!!!" Eliza shouted. Once she said that the rest of the town followed along.

"BURN THE WITCH, BURN THE WITCH, BURN THE WITCH!!!" the crowd shouted along with her.

"WE MUST CLEANSE THE EVIL!!! CLEANSE IT SO THAT WE ALL WILL BE FREE!!! WE MUST BURN THIS EVIL AND SEND IT TO THE FIREY DEPTHS OF HELL WHERE IT BELONGS!!!" Pastor Flease preached to the crowd.

"NOOO!!!!" Greta screamed as she was kicking and squirming while four farmers dragged her back into town. Eleanor ran to her and tried to break the bonds that held onto her.

"This is not happening, no... Greta please no... NOOOO!!!!!!"

"Ellie, wake up!!!" Greta said. Eleanor finally awoke fully knowing the extent of what she had done.

***

Eleanor burst out from her bed and rushed into the kitchen once again. She had reached for the wine glass which was now warm to the touch. She pressed it to her lips not realizing that it was empty. Behind her, she heard Greta enter the room.

"Where is Jacob?" she asked.

"He left as soon as you slept to help bury the childr—" In a fit of rage Eleanor slammed the bottle down onto the floor and screamed.

"Ellie! What is the matter?" Greta shouted. Eleanor would not dare say what she had seen in her dream. For even she did not know whether or not that dream was just a figment of her subconscious or her future that had yet to come.

"All those kids..." Eleanor spoke as her words turned into weeps of unfathomable sadness. She was no longer in control of her body, she collapsed onto the floor and sobbed once more. Greta embraced her friend as she too was feeling the same emotions she was feeling.

"They are in a better place now Elle, they are with our lord our father," Greta said reassuringly.

"They should be with their mothers!!!" Eleanor shouted as she sobbed once more. Greta held her tighter as she was now becoming more manic by the second. "They should be playing in the woods, they should be out with their fathers learning to hunt, they should be with their mothers who would sing them goodnight. That's where they should be Greta! That's where they should be!!!" The was a silence even Greta knew the truth in her words. Greta then stopped holding onto Eleanor and kneeled directly in front of her. Eleanor's head was bobbed down, she then felt a warm hand tilt her head up so that she and Greta would be looking directly at each other. Much like her eyes Greta's eyes were red and glassy as well.

"Don't you dare blame yourself for this Ellie? You and I both know that if we had known something like this would happen, we would have never used the book on the Flease's right?" Eleanor nodded her head. "That book is evil, and you and I both know what we need to do don't we?" Eleanor had an idea of what she was implying when it came to what Greta wanted to do to the book. "We have to destroy it!" With that said Eleanor wiped the tears off her face and nodded.

They both got up off the floor and marched into the living room where the book was last placed and took it out back where Jacob's shop was. Memories came to Eleanor like a wave the last time she was back here was when Jacob's father showed her and Greta the silver blade he made for the pastor. The same day that she died... It only felt as though it was a couple of days ago. Jacob moved the golden musket his dad had on display in the main room into here. Right over his workbench, *guess he likes to think of his dad while he works,* she thought.

"Why couldn't we have used the fireplace?" Eleanor asked. Greta looked at her with intent. Which gave Eleanor a slight chill.

"This book needs to be eradicated. Nothing should be left of this except dust, and I can think of no better place to send this book right back to hell where it came from." Greta said with fire in her voice. With that said there was a thought of hesitation that came over Eleanor. Like a clarifying thought, one has when one sees another option or an easier solution to one's problems.

"Wait, what if..." she said but stopped when Greta looked at her.

"What?"

"What if there was a way to undo what the book had done?" There was another small silence between the two. In that silence, Eleanor attempted to seize the book. As she did Greta took a couple of steps back.

"Ellie what happened to those kids cannot be undone," Greta stated bluntly.

"But what if it could? I mean think about it we have seen this book do the impossible before why would you think it could not bring back the kids that it affected?"

"Because we don't know what would come of it, think back to last night Ellie. We used the book on the Flease's and that ended up hurting the town more than Eliza and her father. It's too much of a risk." Greta added. As she finished her take on Eleanor's hypothesis, Eleanor could not help but think more about it. *She is right about what the book did, but she also did not consider that if she used the book to help bring the kids back to life whatever darkness that has gripped around the town might be broken. It affected the children the most so if I undo what happened to them there's a chance that I could also save the town as well!* This sudden realization sent chills through Ellie, a little part of her felt as though she had discovered a cure for a disease. The disease of death. As this thought ended Greta had finally lit the blazing fire that Jacob uses for his products, where she intends to incinerate the book once and for all.

"See you in him—" she said before getting cut off by Eleanor hitting her head with a shovel. Greta was now completely unconscious; she had dropped the book out of the fire's reach.

"I'm sorry, Greta but I have to try," Eleanor said as she grabbed the book and her cloak and ran out of the shop.

***

At this point, the sun had just gone down. There was a familiarity with how the town was to Eleanor to how it was when she first came here after she had been brought back. Only this time the fog that covered the town seemed to be much thicker than it was before. Eleanor could make out the outlines of buildings, and dim lights coming from the candles inside as well as the torches that hung outside the buildings as well. Eleanor had to think about where they could have buried the children, it had just occurred to her that she had never actually been to the cemetery before. She had no idea whether it was located in town or outside of it. There was only one person who knew exactly where it was, Jacob. Eleanor expected to see people walking around town at this hour considering what had happened. She remembered when she was a little girl and how a huge storm tore through seven buildings and almost her house where she and Peter were. Eleanor remembered just how busy, and alive the town felt after that disaster. She also remembered how her father helped out as much as possible rebuilding the buildings that did not survive the storm. Tonight the town was empty, somehow it felt more empty than it was when she came back to life. *Where could everyone be?* Eleanor heard murmurs coming from in front of her. As she walked closer to the sound, it grew and grew. Suddenly she felt this chill wash over her back. She quickly turned around and saw nothing. Although there wasn't anybody out here, she felt as though she was being watched. She began to walk closer to where the sound was coming from and she made it to a familiar white building, the church.

All of the windows in the church shot out beams of light into the foggy night. Eleanor could tell now that the entire town had to be in there, which also meant that Jacob had to be in there as well. She moved to the right-hand side of the building and found a couple of boxes for her to step on so that she could look inside. Eleanor could see that Jacob was now speaking on the main podium at the front of the church. The people that were in the crowd earlier were all sitting in the audience. Most of their faces were red by how much they had wept for their children. Jacob looked tired; his shirt had large brown splotches on it from helping dig the graves of the kids. He was also covered in sweat; his skin was glistening, it looked as though he was glowing from how much light there was in the church. Much like the grieving mothers and fathers in the crowd, he too looked as though he had cried, his face was sunken, and his eyes looked dreary. In Eleanor's eyes, it looked as though he had not slept in days, even though they had woken up together earlier this morning.

"Can everyone hear me?" Jacob spoke loudly. There was silence in the crowd as he spoke. "Good now we can begin"

"Where is the pastor shouldn't he be speaking?" Freddrick Redd spoke. The crowd began to mutter once more. Jacob simply raised his hands to quiet down the crowd.

"I will be speaking on the Pastor's behalf,"

"On whose authority?" shouted another voice in the crowd. The crowd now got more riled up. Eleanor did not blame them for how they must be feeling, they had all lost something today. She remembered just before she passed out how the cattle had died. Eleanor looked back at Jacob, and he could not answer the question, he was lost for words. Suddenly the doors of the church swung open and Pastor Flease, Eliza, and her friends all walked in. Eleanor jumped slightly along with everyone else inside.

"Yes blacksmith, on whose authority?" said the Pastor condescendedly. Jacob was still too stunned for words. "Certainly not on God's authority? Because the only voice of God in this town is I." Jacob got off the podium and marched directly in front of the pastor's face. The pastor did not flinch as he approached him, he just gave him a smug sneer.

"You do not speak for the lord! You snake!" With that being said the Pastor whips out his silver blade and points it directly in front of Jacob's face. The crowd gasps at this sudden stroke of violence coming from the Pastor. Jacob looked at him wide-eyed, Eleanor as well. Fury bellowed in

Eleanor's chest as the Pastor flaunted his sword in Jacob's face.

"The only snake that is here is the one who has summoned Lucifer to our town." Silence filled the church like the fog outside. Eleanor felt her heart pounding out of her chest. Not just for Jacob's sake but for hers as well. "Someone among us has conspired with Satan himself and murdered our children!!!"

"Your children? YOUR CHILDREN!!! You mean their children" Jacob said while pointing out into the still quiet crowd. "Have they not suffered enough? Now you speak of—of"

"Witchcraft! Dammit, I speak of witchcraft, and someone here is a part of it!!" The pastor shouts into the crowd, which then starts muttering again. Eleanor knew Jacob was panicked; she would be too if she was in his situation right now. Though Jacob displayed a level head as he spoke again.

"You cannot be serious; you're blaming this on witchcraft?"

"Tell me, blacksmith, how would you explain the dying cattle and crops in nearly everyone's farms? I noticed that the children were not the only living creatures who perished today. How would you explain that?"

"Yeah, tell him!!!" Eliza and her friends added on. The crowd then started asking as well, and the building slowly got louder and louder. Jacob could not speak for he could not logically explain how the cattle as well as the crops to the people. The pastor smiled that smug smile towards Jacob again, he then put his sword back into its holster and marched up to the podium while Eliza and her friends followed behind her. As Jacob turned and looked at the Pastor his eyes caught sight of someone in the window, his eyes bulged as he stared at Eleanor. Who was now waving him to come outside? Jacob looked around and the attention was now off of him and now on the pastor. Jacob carefully walked back to the main entrance of the church and slid outside. Eleanor quickly made her way over to him in the front. They then walked over to one of the huts away from the church so that nobody would see or hear them.

"Have you gone mad! You need to get back to the shop you can't be seen!" Jacob whispered to Eleanor

"I know but Jacob I have a way that we can undo what happened to the village!" Eleanor replied. There was a small silence, the two locked eyes and Jacob's anger seemed to be diminishing.

"What are you talking about? And where's Greta?" he asked.

"She's asleep," she lied. Eleanor did not like lying to Jacob but if he knew how Greta felt about this plan, he would not go along with it. "That does not matter right now just look!" Eleanor showed him the book and his eyes bulged once more.

"ARE YOU--!" Eleanor shushed him as quickly as she could.

"Yes, I know but just listen, this book can do the impossible, what's to say that it couldn't bring the kids back?" Eleanor could see the realization in Jacob's eyes. He now knew that they could save the kids, they were the only ones with the power to do so. Jacob immediately grabbed the closest torch he could find which just so happened to be in front of one of the huts.

"Eleanor Shrowl you are brilliant!!!" Jacob exclaimed in a whisper. He then pulled her in and kissed her. After they exchanged the kiss Jacob grabbed Eleanor's hand and walked out to the woods, the same woods that Eleanor had come from when she had risen from the salt watered pond, and was now the final resting place for the twelve children who had perished.

***

Eleanor's only source of light was the torch Jacob was carrying as they made their way through the woods. However, compared to the last time Eleanor walked through these dense woods she felt more comfortable and safe. This time she was not alone, and this time she was not as helpless as she had been just a couple of days ago. Which in her eyes felt like weeks. Eleanor did everything she could to keep up with Jacob. She was trying to look through the book while also walking with him to where he buried the bodies and used the torch so she could see. She eventually gave up trying to multitask when the wind started to pick up once again. It was when she fully caught up with Jacob did, she realized just how different these woods looked since she had last been there. The fog was now so thick one could cut it with a knife. Eleanor was not sure she was even stepping on the ground it looked as though they were walking on clouds. The last time Eleanor walked through these woods she had the moon be her source of light, the moon was nonexistent right now, the only thing that she could see was Jacob holding the torch and marching along the path to where he buried the children. The wind began to pick up once again, she saw that the fog that she and Jacob were walking on started to whisk and curl as each breath of wind came through. It almost felt as though the woods itself were breathing, like she and Jacob were walking into the mouth of a hungry beast. That was ready to swallow them whole and leave nothing behind to be found. The wind sent chills all over Eleanor, who then gripped Jacob's free arm. She did not realize it until now, but she was shivering fiercely. Jacob stopped walking and pulled her in closer.

"Here," he said as he pulled off his jacket.

"No, you'll freeze" Eleanor insisted. Jacob didn't care, he pulled off his jacket and wrapped it around Eleanor. She blushed as he did so, *such a gentleman* she thought. As that tender moment ended a loud howl echoed through the woods. Eleanor and Jacob held each other tightly as they both heard the crackling of leaves coming from their right, and their left. Jacob moved the torch side to side to see what was there. Sure enough two bloodthirsty wolves formed out of the fog. They growled a vicious and ferocious growl that made Eleanor's insides quiver.

"GET BACK!!!" Jacob shouted as he tried his best to scare off the wolves. Eleanor did not know what to do to help her, she was frozen she tried her best to encourage Jacob but all it did was make the wolves all the more angry. They pounced around the flame as if they were dancing in a ballroom. Jacob kept swinging at the wolves as they growled and snarled and attempted to bite them both. Eleanor thought back to the book as Jacob was now fighting for both their lives. Eleanor flipped through the pages trying to find some sort of spell that they could use to defend themselves with. However, it was challenging considering not only did she have to look through this book but she also had to be aware of the wolves close by and the torch (her only light source) was being thrashed around the wolves. She then settled on a spell she liked and decided to use it.

"Kamarro!!!" she shouted, instantly the wolves collided with each other, and there was a loud thump as they both were knocked unconscious.

"What did you do?" Jacob asked still huffing deeply from the fight that just happened. Eleanor snatched the torch from Jacob's hand and marched a few steps over the unconscious dogs.

"I saved our lives, Now let's go save some more," Eleanor said as she pressed forward with Jacob following behind her.

***

They had walked for another thirty minutes *how far did they bury these kids?* After what felt like another hour of walking Eleanor jumped at the sound of Jacob's voice.

"We're here," Jacob said as he grabbed the torch from Eleanor's hand and pointed it at the ground which then erupted into a large flame. The area where they were seemed vaguely familiar as if she had seen it before. She looked around and in a semicircle were twelve small graves. All of which were different sizes in both width and length. Eleanor heard the rumble of thunder overhead. If they were to do this, they needed to do it now. As the fire illuminated the area they were at more and more Eleanor started to remember where they were. She looked at Jacob who smiled as he knew she knew where they were now.

"Is this?" she asked.

"Yes, this was where I had my gathering almost one year ago" Jacob answered. The memories kept flooding into Eleanor's mind. She remembered the music that was being played and how she and Jacob danced around the fire like they were children again. Most of all she remembered how much she had drank that night and how sick she was. But then another memory came to light that was the night she died when Eliza plunged that dagger into her and dumped her body into the salt-watered pond. Where she had lost an entire year of her life. Where she lost her family, her brother. Eleanor could not help but weep solemnly.

"Ellie, what's the matter?" Jacob asked as he held her. Eleanor wiped the tears off her face as she replied.

"It's just the last time I was here I lost so much, I lost almost everything that night. My brother, my family, you and Greta." She said through more tears. Jacob held her tightly as she wept.

"Ellie, do you know why I decided to bury the children here?" Jacob asked. Eleanor shook her head no, as he loosened his hold of her. They both locked eyes as Jacob explained further. "You may see this as the place where you lost everything, but for me, this was the place where I fell in love. Remember how we danced?"

"Yes"

"Ellie I brought these kids here because this place to me is filled with love and joy, and I wanted these kids to be in a place that would not only bring them joy wherever they may be but also the families of those children as well. It's almost as if this place were..."

"Magik" she replied. Jacob nodded as he knew she knew it as well. Eleanor could not believe what she was hearing that was one of the most tenderhearted things she had ever heard in her life. Her heart felt as though it was swimming when she heard Jacob speak. In a way Jacob was right, while Eleanor did lose a lot that night she too felt a burning love come to life that night, that same love that has stuck by her side ever since. This feeling overwhelmed her, warming her up inside and out as she reflected on his words and took what he said to heart. Eleanor looked at her lover with a much deeper connection than she ever thought possible. She slowly walked up to him and kissed him deeply allowing her and his tongue to dance as she knew full-heartedly that Jacob was the one for her.

"I love you, Jacob,"

"And I love you Eleanor" With that being said, Eleanor's heart swooned all over again. She kissed him once more just as the rain began to come down.

***

The rain sprinkled not so much that the fire in the middle of the burial site went out but she needed to hurry if they were going to do this. She flipped through the pages of the book as quickly as she could. She handed Jacob his jacket back so that they could use it to cover the rain. Eleanor eventually found a page she did not recognize. This page had a large back and red flame on it and in the flames was writing. The other pages were more of a list of spells but something about this page seemed to be different. In the flames, it said:

To bring back those who have been lost speak true the words of Rednaxela, Eelos, and Samoht

Verticus Klatos Delifushstro

Three times for each barrier of the mortal realm

"This is it Jacob! This is it!!!" Eleanor shouted in excitement. She looked at Jacob who had a sense of both excitement and hesitation on his face. "What's wrong?" she asked.

"Eleanor, I don't know if this is a good idea," he said. Eleanor looked at him confused. *He was just on board about this plan a second ago what changed?*

"What? Why! We have the spell, we're here why shouldn't we give these kids a second chance!" There was a small silence, the rain began to pick up once more as well as the thunder brewing.

"Eleanor look at that picture! Look at those names those names do not sound human"

"Who cares! I am undoing what I did and then we are going to get the hell out of Florence once and for all!!!" She shouted. Jacob was now left speechless once again. He looked at Eleanor with both fear and bewilderment in his eyes. "Verticus Klatos Delifushstro" she muttered. With each word she spoke the storm began to pick up more and more the wind became so powerful it knocked Eleanor back a couple of steps. The thunder crashed and crackled throughout the sky.

"Ellie..." Jacob said. She did not listen her mind was already made up. She spoke once more.

"Verticus Klatos Delifushstro," she said again. As she did she saw the fire in the middle of the burial site grow twice its size. The rain did not seem to bother the mighty flame as it grew taller than Eleanor. The wind howled and whipped in every direction. Lightning began to illuminate the sky Eleanor looked around and saw how it created shadows along the trees around her. Her eyes stopped wondering about her surroundings when she looked directly beside Jacob was Greta holding a large ax.

"ELLIE STOP!!!" Greta shouted. Eleanor did not realize it but she was now no longer in control of her actions. She raised her hand and flicked the air which sent Greta flying backward and pinned to a tree like a nail on wood.

"GRETA!!!" Jacob shouted as he charged after Eleanor. She too flicked the air and sent him flying ten feet away. He looked up at her in horror he could not move, nor could Greta. Eleanor smiled at both of them as she spoke once more.

"It's all right, I'm going to make everything better," Chills ran through both Greta and Jacob as this was not the voice of Eleanor Shrowl this was someone else, some*thing* else. This voice was much deeper and scratchy, it made their bodies tingle and vibrate with every syllable it spoke.

"No..." Jacob spoke to himself.

"Verticus...klatos...delifushstro"

***

As the last words were spoken a great bolt of lightning erupted from the sky and struck the fire that was in the middle of the burial site. This sent Eleanor flying backward just as far as she had flung Jacob. Eleanor now had full control over herself, and so did Greta and Jacob. The three of them huddled together and clutched each other tightly. The great fire suddenly changed green which none of them had ever seen before. The fire looked as though it was alive. It swerved and bobbed it looked as though it was studying them, the fire looked as though it had turned to see the graves that were laid all around it. Without hesitation, Eleanor grabbed the book and held it tightly in her arms. The fire split into twelve long beams which were connected to the main fire in the middle. Each green beam of fire plunged itself into the ground where the graves were. The ground and the headstones were now lit ablaze into smaller green flames. The wind was now at its top speed, yet nothing was blowing this fire out, not even the rain did anything to stop it. Eleanor had tried to move but the wind was so powerful that she could barely move her arms let alone open her eyes fully. Eleanor felt the ground shift and rumble through her fingers. She looked around and saw the trees begin to shake and rattle from the wind. The sound of thunder was so loud it felt as though the earth was going to split in half. Eleanor's ears began to ring slightly because of how loud it was. She then felt something pull the side of her shirt. It was Greta screaming though she could not hear her screams, she was pointing at the graves. Eleanor screamed when she saw that the children were now coming out of their graves. However, these did not look like the innocent children that perished. The children's skin was now grey and dry, their eyes were bleak red almost crimson. Their clothes were tattered and torn up and were now covered in mud. In the glow of the fire, Eleanor could see that a couple of them had bugs crawling across their faces. Which were still stained with blood from earlier. She also saw that their teeth had already rotted, they were chomping like animals. As they moved, they jerked and spasmed one of the only things Eleanor could hear was the sound of cracking bones coming from the children. Hungry for their next meal. It didn't take Eleanor long to figure out what they were hungry for.

Jacob got up and grabbed the ax that Greta had dropped. He held it with a defensive stance, slowly the kids began to walk towards them. Jacob swung the ax directly into one of the children's heads. It was a little girl who looked as though she was barely six years old. It struck the right side of the little girl and made a loud crack. Her cheek had completely collapsed in itself. Black ooze splattered across Jacob, Greta, and Eleanor. It was as if the blood of this creature had become molasses. Both Eleanor and Greta screamed once again as the little girl did not go down. Instead, the ax just stuck there, the three of them stared blankly as the little girl slowly pulled the ax from out her face. The girl then dropped the ax and stared back at them. The right side of her face was now open completely. Eleanor was able to see her molars through her cheek which flapped off her face like it was a thin slice of meat. The wind began to slow down, she was able to hear more clearly now. The fire slowly changed back into the small flame it was before. Rain came down much harder this time around, it quickly killed the fire. Thunder and lightning illuminated the sky as they stood there in stunned silence. All of the children were now staring at them, their red eyes pierced through them like daggers. They stood there in silence by what they had done for a solid ten seconds. This was not what Eleanor envisioned when she thought of bringing the children back. She was hoping that they would return the way they were before. Instead, they were now walking corpses.

SNAP

Eleanor looked beside her, and Greta had taken a step back right on a twig. The children all let out a horrible scream that echoed throughout the forest for miles. It was unlike anything they had heard before. Eleanor thought that was what the devil sounded like. The ground before them rumbled as the children screamed. Around her, Eleanor saw tree branches and smaller trees fell over because of the intensity of their wails. Ringing came back to Eleanor's ears only this time it was not as intense as before, because she was able to cover her ears. The last thing that Eleanor heard before the children charged towards them was Jacob screaming.

"RUN!!!!"

***

Eleanor did not stop running for a second, not even to look around. She could tell that Greta and Jacob were running alongside her because she could hear them huffing along with her. She could also hear behind her the zombified children she had brought back sprinting towards them. As small as these creatures were Eleanor felt as though they were close, she could hear the pitter-patter of their feet racing through the forest. Her heart was pounding, so much so that it felt as though it was going to beat right out of her chest. Not once in her life has, she ever had to run this fast in her life until now. Not even when she was little and playing with her father or Greta when they were younger. It's a miracle that she and the others have not hit any trees or unseen trenches. The only light that they have is the illuminated stormy sky. Which Eleanor partially spawned upon them. However, in Eleanor's defense, the storm was just starting when she began chanting the words. *Why did I do it? You know why, you thought everything would be alright if you brought them back. You thought that somehow the people would forget all about what happened to them, and everything would be all right again. Well now they are back and now they're monsters. Monsters that are now chasing us, three grown adults through the woods as if we were deer being hunted and mounted.* The storm above crashed as they made their way through the forest. As they ran through the forest Eleanor saw a small light, a familiar light. A light she had seen before recently. The others had seen this light as well and ran towards it without question. As they rushed to the light Eleanor quickly realized where she was. She was back at Delilah's cabin where she was taken after she had woken from her year-long slumber.

"Quick inside!!!" Eleanor shouted as they rushed to the cabin. Jacob was at the front of the pack and without knocking or warning he slammed into the door which gave way by his strength. The three of them managed to get inside the cabin and slammed the door behind them. The zombified children were now at the cabin as well desperately clawing and scratching at the doors and windows. The only thing keeping them at bay was Jacob's raw strength being held against the door. Which was not going to hold long at this rate.

"A little help?" Jacob pleaded. Both Eleanor and Greta both pressed their weight against the door as well. Adrenaline flooded Eleanor's mind at this moment because if they were to falter in any way against the door, they would all be dead. Suddenly a large zombified hand burst through the door and grabbed Eleanor by her hair. She screamed violently as she could see the horrifying creature which now had a literal death grip on her hair. Greta seized from her helping hold the door down to try and help Eleanor, which put more strain on Jacob. Eleanor grabbed hold of Greta's hands as she pulled and tugged desperately trying to loosen the grip on the creature's hand around Eleanor's hair. Pain shot through Eleanor's scalp as this creature lashed her head around like a child playing with a toy. She could feel the hair slowly being ripped off as Greta tried to help her. After what felt like an eternity of agony the creature's grip loosened and the banging on the cabin slowly went away. Greta was able to pull Eleanor away from the door and Jacob was able to move. He looked out at the hole where the arm had grabbed Eleanor.

He turned to the girls with a confused look on his face. "They're gone they're going back up the trail."

"What? Are you sure?" Greta asked.

"See for yourself" Jacob replied. Both Eleanor and Greta peeked through the hole and sure enough, Jacob was right, the children were heading back up the trail they had come from. Confusion overwhelmed the three of them. The creatures could have easily taken them, but they didn't why? It didn't take long for Eleanor to come to a horrifying realization as to why they would leave.

"Oh God…" she spoke to herself.

"What?" Jacob asked.

"The village… all those people…" she replied. Both Greta and Jacob's eyes bulged as they too realized exactly where the children were going.

"We've got to warn them," Jacob said.

"Jacob they won't listen to you, you saw how they treated you as soon as Mr. Flease walked in."

"They'll have to believe me otherwise they'll be dead we have to do something we can't just let them die."

"WHY NOT? WHAT HAVE THOSE PEOPLE EVER DONE FOR US?" Greta shouted. Both Jacob and Eleanor were stunned by shock at what she said.

"Greta, how can you say that?" Eleanor said.

"Oh I'm out of line says the woman who tried to bring back what was dead and look how that ended Ellie"

"I was trying to help the town and give those kids another chance at life Greta they did not deserve what happened to them." Eleanor retorted.

"And because of you more people are going to meet a fate worse than death thanks to you" Greta added. Without hesitation, Eleanor slapped Greta across the face. There was a small silence as Eleanor realized what she had done. Greta wiped a small bit of blood off her lips and pounced on Eleanor. The two were now engaged in a full-fledged fight.

Greta had grabbed the same chunk of hair that Eleanor had just grabbed at by the children. She let out a scream as she punched Greta in the gut. She let out a girthy grunt as she tossed and turned on the floor. The two were then pulled apart by Jacob still kicking and screaming at each other.

"STOP IT BOTH OF YOU!!!!" he shouted. "WE ARE ALL TO BLAME FOR THIS, THERE IS NO POINT IN US BLAMING EACH OTHER!" Both Eleanor and Greta knew that he was right. Yet the resentment they both have towards each other is still present between them. "I am not going to sit by and watch as my town is destroyed, you two stay here and I am going to help out however I can."

"Jacob I—"

"You stay here Ellie... You've done enough" he said. His words cut deep into Eleanor's heart. She knew that most of this was her fault, even though she had good intentions behind her actions. "When I get back, we are leaving Florence and heading west, nobody will think to look for us there. Just stay here and I'll be right back" Jacob carefully opened the front door and walked into the woods outside of the path to try and cut off the horde to town. Eleanor watched her beloved maneuver through the woods with both guilt and shame in her heart.

THE COMPLETE WITCHES' TREASURE SERIES

Witches' Treasure

Part 1

The Discovery of Magik

Witches' Treasure

Part 2

A Witch's Tale

Witches' Treasure

Part 3

All Hell Breaks Loose

Milton Keynes UK
Ingram Content Group UK Ltd.
UKHW020253221123
432980UK00018B/1411